SHADOWS AT BOWERLY HALL

Forced to work as a governess after the death of her father, Amelia Thorne travels north to Yorkshire and the isolated Bowerly Hall. Charles, Viscount Bowerly, is a darkly brooding employer, and Amelia is soon convinced that the stately home holds secrets and danger in its shadows. Then a spate of burglaries in the county raises tensions amongst the villagers and servants, and Amelia finds herself on the hunt for the culprit. Can Charles be trusted?

Books by Carol MacLean
in the Linford Romance Library:

CAROL MacLEAN

SHADOWS AT BOWERLY HALL

Complete and Unabridged

LINFORD
Leicester

First published in Great Britain in 2016

First Linford Edition
published 2017

A catalogue record for this book is available
from the British Library.

ISBN 978–1–4448–3186–3

Published by
F. A. Thorpe (Publishing)
Anstey, Leicestershire

Set by Words & Graphics Ltd.
Anstey, Leicestershire
Printed and bound in Great Britain by
T. J. International Ltd., Padstow, Cornwall

This book is printed on acid-free paper

1

Last night I dreamt I was a child again, and my father a young man. The great hall was lit with candles and the first dance had begun. The ladies' dresses rustled as they spun laughing to the music. I awoke, still with the lingering scent of burning beeswax in my memory.

The room was cold, the girl not yet having lit a fire in the hearth, and I shivered. It took a moment to realise where I was. Not at my childhood home, but at Mrs Bidens' house in an unfashionable part of London. She was a dear friend of my mama, and had taken me in until I could find my feet.

I dressed without the help of a maid, and was pleased to manage the task with not too many difficulties. It reminded me that I must have fortitude and learn quickly, for my life had changed almost overnight.

Downstairs, Mrs Bidens was already up. She was dressed in her usual black bombazine with a lace cap covering her grey hair. We sat together for breakfast, although I could find very little appetite. Today I had to leave this sanctuary and travel north into the unknown.

For now, I took a little toast and a small portion of eggs. Mrs Bidens looked concerned.

'I wish I could keep you here,' she said. 'I'm so sorry you have to leave.'

The truth was, she wasn't wealthy. She owned a modest house left to her by her husband, and had a meagre income. It was not enough to support two women. No, it was essential that I earn my living.

'If only your father ...' Her voice trailed away.

'It wasn't his fault,' I was quick to defend him. 'The accounts and the running of the estate had got quite out of hand before he realised his factor was so unreliable.'

'What a pity everything had to be sold. Your uncle seemed adamant that the house must go too, to pay off the debts.'

'Yes, the house has been sold. Uncle Timothy had no intention of living there in any case. He much prefers the London social life.'

'Perhaps if you had had your debutante season ...' Again, Mrs Bidens found it difficult to complete what she wanted to say.

She blamed my father for my situation. What she didn't know, couldn't know, was what a kind and loving father he had been to me. He may have failed to provide me with a coming-out ball, or a London season to hunt for a husband, but in all other ways he had been the perfect parent. He had been so engrossed in his studies that he hadn't seen I had grown up. To be honest, I didn't miss the social whirl my friends had enjoyed. Being of a shy, retiring nature, I was happy to stay at home with Papa, helping him gather his shells and plants in the countryside nearby.

But Papa had been dead a year. A long year in which I had lived with my Aunt

Lucy and Uncle Timothy. I was not made welcome. Indeed, it was made plain to me that I was a burden to them. When the legal knot surrounding Chelmley Wood had finally been unravelled, my uncle took me aside and told me that I had to find work. I could no longer stay with them.

So here I was with dear Mrs Bidens. It had been wonderful staying these last few weeks with her. I had never known my mama, but Mrs Bidens was able to tell me stories about her and the fun the two friends had shared growing up. What a contrast she was to Aunt Lucy's sour face and bitter tongue!

'I do hope this position works out for you,' my dear friend was saying.

I pulled myself away from my musings and back to the present moment. 'I'm sure it will do very nicely,' I said with a smile, while my stomach flipped painfully.

'I haven't seen Anne for many a year, but her granddaughter is of an age now to need a governess. I see God's hand in this, for you must have a place to live and work. Bowerly Hall is a gorgeous house, if a little … isolated. That part of Yorkshire is rather exposed to the weather. You must wrap up warmly. The summer is almost done.'

'And what of Mary's father?' What of the Viscount himself, my new employer?

'Charles?' Mrs Bidens frowned. 'I remember him as a boy being rather solemn; but of the man he has grown into, I cannot say. He is a widower, as you know. I daresay he finds it rather difficult looking after a small child of seven. Which is lucky for you, my dear. As Mary's governess, you will have a position at Bowerly Hall and a roof over your head for a few years. A measure of security for a long while.'

And after that? I could not think further than my new life at Bowerly. What life would bring when Mary was grown, I had no idea. For the moment, though, I would have employment, board and lodging, and a small monthly salary.

There were tears on both sides as I boarded the train to York. I waved until Mrs Bidens' figure grew tiny and vanished from sight. Then I was truly alone. The knowledge of this gripped me and my throat tightened. The mournful hoot of the steam engine echoed my feelings. To distract myself, I unpacked the basket Mrs Bidens had given me to see what food there was for lunch. It was an odd thought that, by the time I ate it, I would be far away from London. Far away from the familiar south. Chelmley Wood, nestled in the gentle South Downs, flashed in front of my eyes, until I put it from me firmly. That part of my life was finished. Now I had to look ahead to the north.

My bones ached by the time I had finished my journey. First the train, with its smoky taste of coal and ever-rattling windows; then the crowded stagecoach; and finally a lift on a farmer's cart. The old man tipped his hat as I clambered off, my luggage at my feet. Soon he too was out of sight.

I was glad of my thick layers of petticoats. The wind was whipping up around me, a few early autumn leaves twirling in the air. I hugged my shawl closer. Ahead of me, through the hedgerows and the gathering dusk, I saw Bowerly Hall. It was a great grey block of a house. A sombre square looming over the fields beyond. No finesse, no charming curlicues of stone carvings nor Grecian columns. A plain, sturdy, northern abode. Such were my thoughts as I picked up my bags and walked towards it.

There had been unsettling talk amongst the stagecoach travellers. When they heard where I was going, there were raised eyebrows and a few exchanged glances. One woman, a lively gossiping type, told me why. Apparently there had been a spate of thefts in the county. When I remarked that I couldn't see how that would affect me, her gaze slid quickly away. I felt it to be a nonsense. She was the sort who liked drama, I decided.

When I reached the house, I had a dilemma. Was I to enter through the front door? Or was I to present myself at the servants' entrance? To be a governess was to be neither fish nor fowl. It would be down to the family and how they perceived me. I hoped very much to be accepted by all within Bowerly.

Luckily, as I hesitated, a small figure came running out of the main door. It was a little girl, quite thin and pale-faced but her eyes sparkled and she had a wide smile for me.

'You must be Mary,' I said.

Her mouth opened in surprise. 'How did you know that? I know that you are Miss Amelia Thorne because my grand-mamma has told me. Will you come inside with me and meet her?'

She took my hand with sweet childish confidence, and so I was drawn inside the rather gloomy house. A footman took my luggage and indicated I should go to a room immediately to my left. Mary led the way. My heart was pounding with nerves, but I needn't have worried. The dowager Viscountess rose from her chair and came towards me with a welcoming smile.

'Amelia, how lovely to see you at last. Hannah Bidens didn't do you justice when she wrote with her descriptions.

You are a very attractive young woman. Such raven hair, it's rather unusual with those light grey eyes. You are very like your mother. Except she was a little taller, I think.'

'You met my mother?' I whispered. I couldn't believe my luck. Perhaps Lady Anne would have stories to tell me.

'Indeed I did. It was many years ago, of course, when I went visiting with Hannah. Your mother was her playmate, and the three of us had a merry time. But we can talk of this later. Right now I must call for tea. You look exhausted. Come and sit with me.'

'Will there be cake?' Mary piped up smartly.

Lady Anne looked at her sternly, but there was a twinkle in her gaze that told me she was fond of the child, 'It is past your bedtime, Mary. You may stay for a moment to greet Miss Amelia, and have a tiny slice of cake, but then you must go upstairs before your papa returns.'

At the mention of her father, Mary looked rather frightened. Her worried look infected me. I felt my stomach twinge. What kind of man was he? Would he be happy that I was here? It was vital that I keep this job. I had nowhere else to go.

I touched the cameo brooch at my throat. It was my talisman. My mother had left it in her will to me for when I came of age. It was one of the few things Papa had remembered to carry out correctly. On my eighteenth birthday, I had received the brooch and a few pieces of her jewellery. I prayed I would never need to sell them.

'I hope you will be happy here, Amelia,' Lady Anne was saying. 'Charles has left the organisation of a governess for Mary very much to me. He is busy with running the estate and breeding fine horses. You will teach Mary some reading, writing and arithmetic, of course. I would also like her to learn to paint watercolours. Do you speak French?'

I nodded. I did indeed speak French, and was glad that my father had educated me well. Besides French, I had a good knowledge of botany and geology from helping with his studies, and I thought how nice it might be to teach Mary a little of those subjects on milder days in spring and summer. I began to warm to my task. Hopefully, tutoring would come easily to me.

'There is not much here in the way of entertainment for a young lady,' Lady Anne said, 'I hope you won't find living here too lonely. It is rather an out-of-the-way property, but that is how Charles and I prefer to live. We go to London in the summers, of course, but you will stay here with Mary.'

I assured her that I would not be lonely, and hoped that was true. I enjoyed reading and writing and country walks. Those would have to be enough. I didn't much care for London, and could live without parties and balls.

Once we had chatted, Mary was sent upstairs in the company of a maid, and I was shown by the same footman to my rooms. There was a large bedroom which was to be mine. It was prettily decorated in yellow and pale lemon, and had a fireplace in which a small fire was crackling. Despite the fire, the room was chilly. I wasn't used to the cold north yet. The window looked out to the back of the house, and to the grey sea in the near distance. It would be fun to take Mary down to the beach, I decided. She was such a sickly-looking child, some fresh air would be of benefit.

An adjoining door linked my bedroom to a pleasant sitting room. Again, a lit fire graced the room and made it cosy. I could imagine myself spending quiet hours here with embroidery or books, or perhaps entertaining a friend — should I make any.

At that moment there was a knock on the door. I called out to whoever it was to come in. A tall, thickset woman in middle age entered.

'Miss Thorne? I am Mrs Dane, the housekeeper. I came to introduce myself, and tomorrow you can meet the rest of the staff.'

'How do you do, Mrs Dane,' I said politely, and extended my hand to shake hers.

She was awkward then. Was it my cultured accent that put her off? Had she been expecting a girl of lower birth? It was possible. There were many young women from both gentle birth and the middling classes who desperately needed work. I was keen to put her at ease.

'I haven't met Viscount Bowerly yet. What is he like?'

If I had hoped to put her at ease, it had the opposite effect. She pursed her lips as if she would say nothing, and then made a visible attempt at relaxing.

'Lord Bowerly is a good employer. He is fair in his dealings with the staff, and that is all we need to know.'

I felt I had been rebuffed and put firmly in my place. I wasn't sure what to say next.

'You will wish to take your meals in your sitting room.' Mrs Dane filled the silence. 'I will arrange that with Cook. Do you have everything you need?'

I opened my mouth to protest. I did not want to take my meals in my room; I wanted to eat in company. Yet she had made it quite clear that I was expected to do so. Was I not to be welcome downstairs in the servants' domain? The hope of making new friends died like a flame snuffed out.

'Yes, thank you, I have all I could ask for.'

She nodded swiftly and left me there, shutting the door on her exit. The closed door seemed an omen. I had never felt so lonely. Papa had entertained friends only seldom at Chelmley Wood, but I never felt the lack of company there. It was sufficient to be with him. Here, there was no-one.

I felt myself sink into self-pity, and at once I straightened my back. I lifted my chin and forced a smile to my face. There was no-one to appreciate my stance, but I felt more confident. Bowerly Hall was not going to get the better of me. I had to adapt to my new life. I must make the best of it.

Mrs Dane's words reminded me that I had not had any dinner. It was dark outside and rather late. There was a bell to pull to summon a servant, but I didn't dare use it. No, I would walk downstairs and find the cook instead.

There was no-one about as I tread softly down the stairs. I had no idea where the servants' hall was, and my intention was to explore the ground floor until I found a staircase to it, or to ask the nearest footman. I didn't want to intrude on Lady Anne. She had been very kind to me, but I must not assume a familiarity which might not exist.

I had stepped out into the wide hallway when a door was flung open nearby and a man came striding out. He hadn't seen me, and I saved myself by jumping backwards. His onward movement halted.

I stared up at him. He was so tall. At least a foot taller than me. His thick hair was almost as dark as my own, and I was aware of two burning blue eyes ranging over me. He was dressed impeccably for dinner. Before he spoke, I knew that this must be Charles, Lord Bowerly.

'Forgive me,' he said, in a clipped tone which rather indicated his disinterest in whether I did or not. 'I did not see you there in the shadows.'

'It is of no matter,' I said, but my heart beat fast and my cheeks felt hot.

'You must be Miss Thorne, Mary's new governess. My mother will have spoken with you?'

'Yes, thank you.' I mouthed the words politely while I took surreptitious note of him. He had sharp, high cheekbones and a long patrician nose. A strong jaw indicated determination, and his shoulders a powerful physique. Overall I had the impression of a hawk: as if nothing escaped his notice. This impression was proved false when he spoke about his daughter.

'You will find Mary a healthy child with too much energy. I'm told she must be curbed for her own good. A strict education fit for a girl is what I wish you to provide, Miss Thorne.'

Healthy? Poor Mary looked anything but healthy. She was far too white and thin. As for 'curbing her energy', what did this mean? Who had told him that?

16

He didn't appear to know his own child.

'An education, at any rate.' I smiled. Leaving out the word 'strict'.

He frowned then, a dark glower which made me shrink back. He looked as if he would say more, but instead he turned on his heel and vanished into a nearby room. I interlaced my hands, squeezing the shake from my knuckles. I didn't want anyone to see how he had affected me. I sensed a dark aura around him. It made me afraid.

2

I found the stairway down to the servants' hall and found myself in a long dining room. There was a polished wooden table, and enough chairs to seat quite a number of people. It was empty and silent, but beyond I heard talking. Following the sound, I went into a large kitchen, low-lit by oil lamps and a good range fire. There were two women there. The older one frowned at the sight of me.

'Yes?' she said, rather abruptly.

'I wondered if I might have some dinner.' I smiled politely. 'I arrived this evening. I am to be governess to Miss Mary.'

'I know who you are. I've finished making meals for the family today. There is hot chocolate on the side there. You may help yourself,' she said begrudgingly. She turned to her companion, who was dressed in a maid's uniform. 'Peggy, that's

18

me away. Turn down the lamps and put out the candles before you go for the night.'

Ignoring me, she brushed past me and disappeared, her footsteps slapping on the stone stairs.

Peggy grinned. 'Don't mind Mrs Bell. Her bark's worse than her bite — at least, usually. I can get you some bread and butter to go with your hot chocolate, if you like?'

'Yes please.' I was grateful for her friendliness.

'Have you come far?' Peggy asked as she poured the thick brown liquid from a silver pot into a cup. The sweet aroma made my stomach growl.

'From London,' I said, then asked what was on my mind. 'Mrs Bell seems to have taken against me. I wonder why?'

For a moment, Peggy looked awkward as she spread the butter onto a thick slice of bread and passed the plate to me. 'You mustn't take it personal, like; but you see — Mrs Smith, who was Miss Mary's nanny, is Mrs Bell's cousin.'

'But what has that to do with me?' I was bewildered.

Peggy sat with me as I ate. She was a rosy-cheeked young girl with red curls escaping from her cap. A scattering of freckles graced her nose, and she had the look of someone who laughed often.

'Mrs Smith was let go, and Mrs Bell was very unhappy about that. She says her cousin has not been able to find employment locally and will have to move away.'

'Isn't it normal for the nanny to leave when the child is old enough for a tutor or governess? Miss Mary is seven years old. Too old for a nanny, surely?'

'Mrs Smith hoped to be kept on in another position. I'm sorry to say that Mrs Bell is furious on her cousin's behalf, and she blames you. She thinks that if you hadn't come, Miss Mary would've done with a nanny for longer. His lordship is somewhat ... absent-minded when it comes to his daughter. He might've let things go on the way they were for quite some while. Or so Mrs Bell believes. You coming along has put the cat amongst the pigeons, you see.'

'It's rather unfair,' I said, without thinking. Then I flushed: I didn't want to appear to criticise the cook. After all, I was new here, and I must try to fit in somehow.

But Peggy didn't seem to mind. She chuckled and nodded. 'Aye, it is that. Never you mind. Keep your nose clean, and keep out of Cook's way. You'll be alright.'

I wanted to believe her. At least in Peggy I now had a friendly face amongst the servants. Feeling much better for the food and hot drink, I took my leave of her and stepped quickly back upstairs to my rooms. They already felt like a sanctuary.

★ ★ ★

I awoke the next morning after a most unsettled night. I had wild dreams where dark figures chased me across shadowed landscapes, and I had tossed and turned in twisted sheets until I was exhausted. It took all my resolve to ready myself for the first day of my employment. In reality, I would happily have taken to my bed and slept for hours.

Mary was waiting for me in the nursery. It was all dark wood panelling and high ceilings at the top of the house. The long windows looked out on the back, and had much the same view as mine. I could see meadows and fields and the sea: today, much more blue than grey, and considerably calmer.

'What will I be learning?' Mary asked eagerly. Her little feet danced in excitement, and I thought how lovely it was to have such an attentive pupil.

'Perhaps we might start with spelling,' I said, 'then I will read you a story; and if I am happy with your progress, we will paint with watercolours. What do you think of that?'

Mary was happy with my suggestions and we set to work. The morning flew past and we got along well. My charge was a clever child, quick to understand and to remember all that I taught her.

She had a talent for art, and I felt that she could improve to a good standard if she applied herself to our painting lessons.

I looked up to see that it was midday and the sun was shining brightly outside.

'Let us wash our brushes and tidy up, then we'll have a walk outside for some fresh air,' I said.

Mary looked worried. 'I'm not allowed to play outside.'

'What nonsense, it will do you good.' I wanted to add that she needed a bloom of roses in her cheeks, but stopped myself. 'Besides, we won't be playing, but rather walking, which is very good for both the body and the mind.'

She still looked unconvinced. She bit at her lower lip as if she might cry.

'Mary, what is it?' I asked as my heart went out to her. I put my arm around her thin shoulders and felt her shake. 'Come, tell me what is bothering you. I shall put it right.'

'Nanny said only naughty girls go outside. She said that proper young ladies must stay in and be good and still and silent. I know I was often naughty. Nanny said my mama would not have liked me.'

I gasped. What a terrible thing to say to a young child who was motherless! I gathered her in closer. She rubbed at her wet eyes until I found my handkerchief and urged her to use it.

'I have never met your nanny, but I know for certain that your mother loved you. Every mother loves her child no matter what they do. Don't you think that your mama is watching you from heaven? She knows you to be a lovely girl who is clever and quick with a good heart.'

Mary peeped up at me shyly. I wanted to find Mrs Smith and shake the woman for her evil. What else had she said or done to this little girl? She would have had sole command in the nursery from when Mary was a baby. I doubted that Mary's father would have known what was going on, or Lady Anne. There was no-one to tell them. I couldn't imagine Mrs Dane taking an interest. Certainly Mrs Bell would have been on her cousin's side.

'We shall put on our coats and take a short walk,' I said firmly. 'Some pure, fresh air will do us good. Remember, Mary, I am now in charge of you, and I want you to be as happy and industrious as you can be. That will please your grandmamma and your father very much.'

Mary managed a smile. I helped her on with her soft blue velvet coat and matching bonnet. Although the sun was shining, I knew it would be cool outside. I fetched my own coat, glad of its good quality, and took Mary's hand. She clutched at me tightly, and my chest warmed. I was already fond of my charge. Her light blonde hair was very pretty, and her brown eyes had lost their tears. I wondered if she took after her mother in looks, for there was nothing of her father's darkness in her.

We walked from the back of the house, across the formal lawn and through the walled kitchen garden until we were out onto the meadows I had glimpsed from the nursery window. The air smelt sweet with the fading blooms of campion and knapweed. Mary soon livened up enough to skip beside me. It was a fair stretch between Bowerly Hall and the sea, but I enjoyed the exercise and the sense of freedom. Here, I could for a moment forget the tensions of the house and its staff. Although, glancing back, I noticed a face at the window on the second storey. Whoever it was stepped back quickly. I did not know if it was a man or a woman, family or servant. However, I soon forgot my unease as a light breeze ruffled our skirts, and Mary laughed and tried to catch the falling leaves from the scattered trees.

Ahead of us were two figures. As we neared, I saw one was a young woman, perhaps my age or slightly older. The other was a child. Mary hesitated when the girl turned and waved. I pushed the small of her back gently.

'Go,' I said, 'a playmate is waiting.'

Mary shook her head. 'I'm not allowed to play with the village children. If I see them when we go to church, I must turn my head away.'

I sighed. No doubt this was Nanny's

stern advice once more.

'There can be no harm in being nice to this girl,' I said. 'I am right behind you. Go on, now.'

Reluctantly, she walked forward. The other child ran to her. She had a red ball and began to throw it high in the air and catch it. Every time she did so, she giggled. Mary watched until the girl threw it to her. She caught it nimbly, and soon they were laughing and playing together. The young woman approached me.

'Good afternoon. I'm Sarah Wyckham, from the vicarage. You must be Miss Mary's new governess.'

News travelled fast, I supposed, in small places like Bowerly.

'Yes, I'm Amelia Thorne. Pleased to make your acquaintance.'

Sarah was taller than me, with brown hair just visible under a large bonnet. Her clothes were neat and clean, but not fashionable. I didn't judge her on this. My own clothes would soon lose their fashion. I could hardly afford new fabric, nor a dressmaker to make me gowns.

'Are you going to the beach?' Sarah asked.

'I had thought to do so, but it's further away than it looks from the house.'

'Do be careful of the cliff edge,' she warned, 'the meadows end rather suddenly, and there is no wall nor hedge between the grass edge, and a very long drop down to the rocks.'

I shuddered, and realised I must keep a good grip on Mary if we ventured so far.

'You must come and visit me at the vicarage,' Sarah said. 'I would be glad of your company. My father is very busy — particularly now, with the problems at Whitehaven Castle. It's rather lonely without him to fuss over, and when he comes home he's so tired he doesn't wish to talk.'

I warmed to her. It was nice to be invited out somewhere, and I knew I would visit her. She sounded as if she had the same relationship with her father as I had had with mine.

'What has happened at the castle to keep him so busy?' I asked.

She frowned, and I thought she wouldn't answer. She spent a minute gazing at the two children who were skipping together through the long grass.

'Forgive me,' I said quickly. 'It's none of my business. I wasn't meaning to be nosey.'

'It isn't that.' Sarah smiled. 'I don't want to be a gossip. I'm not saying anything that isn't known around the county though. There was a theft at Whitehaven Castle last week and the culprits made off with a hoard of the family's valuable paintings and jewellery. The family is naturally very upset and my father has been supporting them.'

'How awful,' I said, thinking of the chatter and rumours voiced by the travellers on the stagecoach. It was true, then. Thieves were at large in the countryside around Bowerly Hall. I felt a prickle up my spine. Then I shook myself mentally. Goodness, it wasn't as if we were going to be attacked in broad daylight! Besides, what did I have that a thief would want? I had very little in the way of worldly goods. Uncle Timothy and Aunt Lucy had made sure of that. Anything of value at Chelmley Wood had gone, with the house itself, to pay my father's debts. I was left with my clothes, my mother's small pieces of jewellery, and a few of Father's books that I had managed to sneak into my bag. They were worth nothing financially, but to me they were of priceless emotional value. I could see his finger marks on the pages and his scribbled notes in the margins querying a plant name or a geological fact.

'It is awful,' Sarah was saying in agreement. 'It isn't the first in the county, either. You know, they brought a detective all the way from London to investigate, but he's gone back down south now. He found no clues or suspects at all.'

'How strange. Whoever is carrying out the terrible deeds must be very clever and bold.'

'Yes, and very wicked too.'

'I do hope Bowerly Hall is safe,' I said. 'It is quite a distance from any other house.'

Sarah touched my arm reassuringly. 'I'm sure the hall will be fine. After all, it's home to such a lot of people, it's hard to imagine how a thief could gain entry without being noticed.'

And yet, this was what must have happened at Whitehaven Castle and the other places that had been burgled.

I took a deep breath. It was too nice a day to dwell on dark subjects and fears. Especially when in reality they had nothing to do with me. No, my focus must be entirely on Mary.

'Goodness, it's getting late,' Sarah said. 'I must take Charlotte home. It's been lovely to meet you, and please do come and visit with us. Promise me?'

'I promise,' I told her warmly.

Mary and I waved as Sarah and Charlotte left the meadows. Mary was excited and flushed.

'Charlotte is two months older than me. She knows all the names of the birds in the trees. Isn't that marvellous?'

'That is indeed marvellous. But you could learn them too, if you want to. We can bring a notebook next time and write down what we see on our walk. Would you like to do that?'

She nodded vigorously. 'Oh, yes please, Miss Amelia. Did you know that Charlotte has a bear at home with real fur? And she has a doll that belonged to her mother.'

She chattered at my side as we walked further on, and I hid a smile. There was clearly some hero-worship going on. Charlotte was the most wonderful girl ever born, if you listened to Mary. I decided it could do no harm. Charlotte's human flaws would be revealed in due course, and Mary must learn to deal with them then. I hoped very much that a friendship would develop between them. Mary was as isolated as Bowerly Hall itself, and I wanted to change that for her. Besides, hadn't I too made a friend that day? Sarah was a friendly, warm person, and I was looking forward to meeting her again. I too was happier. First Peggy and then Sarah had been kind to me. My life at Bowerly was looking more positive.

'Are we going onto the beach?' Mary asked.

I looked ahead. Sarah was right. The meadows, with their softly waving grasses and seed heads, came to a stop as if a line had been drawn between the green grass and the blue sky. It was impossible to see the drop off the cliffs.

'I'm not sure we can get to the beach,' I said. 'Unless we can find a path down somehow. Let's go and see. Keep a very good hold of my hand, Mary, and don't let go.'

The breeze was growing stronger as we approached the cliff edge. It was blowing directly off the sea. In it, I felt an autumnal chill. I didn't want to approach too closely. The grass was slippery and the whole edge dangerous. We walked in parallel as I searched for a path or a set of steps to the beach.

Ahead of us, I saw a break in the grass and a block of chalky white grit. Could this be the path? Before we had time to investigate, there came the thudding of hooves. I pulled Mary round with me to face the rider.

It was Charles, Lord Bowerly, on the back of a great black horse. Mary pressed right into my side. I noted his excellent seat on the beast, that of an experienced rider, and the firm strength by which he kept control of the bit between his mount's teeth.

I opened my mouth to greet him but he spoke first.

'What the devil do you mean by walking here?' he said, his voice raised and stern above the sound of the breaking waves nearby.

'Why should we not?' I replied, failing to keep the indignation from my tone.

He looked surprised that I should answer him so. I was a little surprised myself. I knew that I should have given in to him politely, yet my anger rose at his rude arrogance.

'You will take my daughter home immediately,' he ordered.

'She is not in any danger,' I said. 'We were merely trying to find a way down to the beach.'

His dark brows met and my heart raced. He was not a man to be trifled with. He was my employer and a Viscount. I was simply the governess. I told myself to remember my place. If only my emotions could follow the logic of my head!

'I do not wish either of you to come here again,' he said. 'The cliffs and the beach are out of bounds. Now, Miss Thorne, you will do as I wish and return to the Hall.'

He did not wait for an answer, but turned the great black horse and galloped off across the meadows.

3

'My, what an appetite you have, miss.' Peggy grinned as Mary tucked into her late luncheon with verve.

I had asked for eggs and bread, and Peggy had brought them to the nursery. She lingered to chat.

'Peggy, do you know of a way down to the beach from the cliffs?' I asked.

The maid nodded. 'Yes, it's easy enough if you're local. I daresay you missed the stairs, not knowing the area.'

'Stairs?'

She laughed, and her bright curls bobbed under her cap. She pushed them up out of sight and winked at Mary, who giggled and popped another spoonful of egg into her mouth. I was pleased to see such a good appetite after our exertions. She was still pale, but I had high hopes for more such outings, in spite of her father.

'Yes, stairs. Not real ones, of course, like in a house, or nothing. They're made out of stone. Someone a long time ago cut them out. Must've been hard work chiselling them, right enough.'

'Where are they? We walked along the cliff edge, but couldn't find a way down.' I didn't mention that I thought we might have found them just as Lord Bowerly interrupted us. From Peggy's answer, I realised I was right. We had been just about at the top of the chalk 'stairs'.

'But you must be careful, Miss Thorne,' she said, her usual cheerful face for once solemn. 'There's more than one villager lost their lives over those cliffs.'

'But the stairs are safe?' I persisted. I wasn't sure why. Only that it piqued me to be forbidden to go there. Lord Bowerly had given no reason for his command. Unfortunately, that made me only more determined to find the beach and see what the fuss was all about.

'Oh, yes.' Peggy nodded. 'Once you're on the stairs they're wide and flat. There's no rail, but as long as you take them slow, you're fine. The danger is in the cliffs themselves. It's so difficult to see the edge. That's why most folk around here avoid them. There's a much nicer beach a mile or so along the coast. It's flat there, with no horrid rock faces to climb down. On my Sunday off, if it's a dry day, me and my sisters walk there with a picnic; it's lovely, it is.'

I envied her. Although she was a maid, and poorly paid for her drudgery, she had a family to enjoy her leisure hours with. She was rich in the ways that matter.

'Please, Miss Amelia, are there more eggs?' Mary said.

'You've eaten every last one, but we can order more from the kitchen,' I smiled.

Peggy rubbed the back of her neck. 'If I'd known you liked them eggs so much, I'd have asked Cook to make you some long ago. It was always milk puddings every day, that was your favourite.'

Mary made a face. 'I hate milk pudding.'

'It is good for you,' I rebuked her mildly, 'but eggs and vegetables are good too. Now, eat your dessert apple and see if that fills you up.'

I could guess who had ordered the daily milk pudding. Mary's nanny, no doubt. Yet, in this, I couldn't fault her. It was a staple of the nursery diet and of benefit to delicate stomachs. However, I decided that if Mary liked eggs, then eggs she would get from now on. I was glad to see her with an appetite.

The door opened and Mrs Dane came in. Her expression changed from carefully blank to disapproving when she saw Peggy.

'There is dusting to be done in the bedrooms. Go along, now. It won't wait on you all day.'

Peggy scuttled off, eyes downward.

'Can I help you, Mrs Dane?' I asked politely.

Her steely glare didn't waver. 'Lady Bowerly asks for your presence in the drawing room.'

'Thank you.' I followed her ramrod-straight back down the staircase until our paths diverged.

Lady Anne rose gracefully from her chair when she saw me. There was a square of embroidery draped on a small occasional table which she must have been working on.

'Ah, Amelia. How are you settling in? Is everything to your liking?'

I was touched that she should care. I think that the link between her, Mrs Bidens and my dear mother helped. I was deeply aware of the strange division between the family and their staff that I appeared to straddle precariously. Mrs Dane clearly disapproved of me coming to the drawing room to talk to Her Ladyship.

'I am quite content, thank you. Mary is a wonderful little girl, and I am sure we shall get along very well in our lessons.'

She looked mildly surprised at my enthusiasm. I realised that, despite her obvious fondness for Mary, she probably had little to do with her on a daily basis. I knew that since Mrs Smith had left, it was Peggy's job to get Mary clean and fresh to be presented to Lady Anne and

His Lordship before their dinner. The impression I got from Peggy was that Mary wasn't downstairs very long each day. That didn't mean she wasn't much-loved, I reminded myself. It was simply the way grand families lived. How different it was from my own country upbringing.

'That is very good news indeed.' Lady Anne smiled. 'I hope you will be happy here, Amelia.'

She sat down in the armchair and picked up her embroidery. I hesitated, unsure whether I had been dismissed or not. She looked up as if she had remembered something else she wanted to say. 'It is good for Mary to take walks. Do not venture too far from the house, however.'

Once more my obstinate streak rose up and refused to be silenced.

'I thought she might enjoy gathering shells on the beach,' I said.

Lady Anne shook her head. 'There is no way down to the near beach from the grounds, and the next beach is quite some distance to walk. Mary must be content with the meadows where she can pick flowers. Bowerly Woods are pleasant, too, for walking.'

I bent my head as if in agreement to her wishes. As I hurried back upstairs to the nursery, my mind spun. Lady Anne had lied to me. There was a stone staircase down to the beach. Peggy had told me so. And had I not seen the very top of it with my own eyes? Why, then, should Lady Anne try to divert me away from the truth? I thought again of the pale face watching me from the Hall, and shivered.

Mary's high spirits had wilted by early evening, and I did not suggest another walk outside. Besides, there was a cold wind which rattled the window casings and caused a mournful howl as it wrapped itself around Bowerly Hall's chimneys.

Instead, we took out our painting materials and tried to recreate the fading summer meadow. I saw that Mary's picture included four people, and guessed she was painting from memory our delightful encounter that day with Sarah and Charlotte. For myself, I experimented with blues and greys, and ended up with a stormy sky and dark-streaked grass. Not quite the happy image I had intended.

The rest of the evening passed peacefully, and I was glad to take a candle and find my way to bed. I hoped for a deep slumber and to waken refreshed, but it was not to be. I lay awake, staring at the ceiling. The wind had died down and the house was silent apart from the creak of old wood settling.

I must have finally drifted off, because all of a sudden I was startled awake. But by what? My head was fogged with sleep. I rubbed my eyes and sat up. There was a noise. I waited. There it came again. Was it the faint sound of hooves?

I slid out of bed and went to the window. It was a deep velvet black outside. I pressed my face to the glass, and my sight adjusted to the darkness. It was enough to make out an impression of movement. Who was down there? Why was someone out and about in the middle of the night?

Curiosity burned in me. Without thinking further, I put on my coat and boots and slipped out of my room. My thoughts floated like strips of ribbon in air. Was someone ill? Could it have been the doctor's horse I had heard? Or perhaps a footman sent to fetch him from the village? A visitor arriving late at the house?

I arrived in the empty hallway convinced that I could help in some way — only to find no-one there. At this point, I should have gone back to bed. But I wanted to know what was going on. The front door was unlocked, and I thought how odd that was. If there were thieves about, it would be only too easy for them to gain access to Bowerly.

Yet, strangely, it did not occur to me that I was in any danger. Instead, I found myself energised and eager to go outside. My life was otherwise so calm and without event. Here was something new.

It was very cold outside as the blackness enveloped me. The air smelt sharp and salty as if it had come straight from the sea. After a moment, I could make out the square of lawn in the moonlight;

ahead of me, the shadow of the wall from the kitchen garden. I hurried towards it. There was no sound of hooves now. No movement. I stopped, confused. Had I imagined it all?

There could be no harm in walking a little further to the edge of the meadow, I decided. It was exhilarating being out at such a late hour. I looked back at the sleeping house. There were no lights in any of the windows. It struck me that perhaps I was looking in the wrong place. I had heard a horse's hooves — or so I thought. I should go to the stables. I wavered between my desire to see the meadow in the moonlight, and the logic of visiting the stables first. I knew they lay on the far side of Bowerly, although I had not yet been inside them.

I was almost through the kitchen garden now. I decided to go just beyond to see the meadow before retracing my steps. As I did so, I gasped. There was a flicker of orange light far ahead, just where the meadow met the cliffs. It was so tiny I might have missed it. The moon was covered by cloud, and I could not make out any figures. The single bobbing glow was unnerving, as if a ghost were abroad ...

I shook myself angrily. What nonsense! It was perhaps a natural phenomenon such as a will-o'-the-wisp of gas. I knew these to occur in marshes, though not on grass. However, I still had much to learn about the world. It was not inconceivable that nature was to blame for what lay ahead of me. The alternative was that someone was awake, just like me. Awake and heading for the beach ... The light had disappeared over the edge of the cliff. Peggy's description of the stone stair came back to me. I judged it to be in the right area where the light had been.

I walked swiftly through the dew-laden grasses. A sweet scent of hay and per-fumed petals stirred wherever my feet trod. Overhead, an owl hooted, and glided past on whispering wings. Something small rustled beside me. A small creature hiding from the bird, no doubt. I picked up my pace. Whoever it was in front of me had a few minutes' grace. If I lingered here in this magical place, I might lose them.

Soon I had reached the lip of the cliffs. The moonlight came and went as the clouds sailed by. One minute, I saw quite clearly; the next, all was cast into gloom. Luckily, the chalky white stone of the top of the stair was bright enough to see. I stood at the top and peered down.

The swell of the sea was faintly visible. I heard the suck and pull of waves hitting the beach. Then I saw the oddest thing. The flame I had followed, which I now presumed to be a lantern of some sort, moved up the cliffs! Again, I thought of ghosts. My heart thudded in my ribcage. Then it simply disappeared. A few orange flickers and it was gone. What was happening?

I put a first nervous foot onto the top step. Gingerly, I stepped down. But Peggy was right. The steps were reasonably broad and flat. There was no reason to fear. I moved carefully and methodically down. The stair was built diagonally into the rock so that, as I descended, I always had the shelter of the rock face to my right. I concentrated on placing my feet. I told myself not to look along the beach, not to search for the lantern. I did not ask myself what I was doing here.

My hair swung heavily into my face and I pushed the long plait back impatiently. The last few steps were slimy with seaweed. I lurched and clutched at the rock. Then at last my feet touched the crunch of sand.

I had barely caught my breath when I became aware of someone running. There was a thudding on the sand. Just as I realised that whoever it was, was coming towards me, I was knocked hard on the shoulder. Crying out, I fell heavily. I tasted the grit in my mouth. The person had not waited to help me to my feet. He or she had not seen me when they pushed by me — no, it was surely a man. A woman would not have such force or bulked strength.

I managed to stand. My legs were shaking. Suddenly, I had had enough adventure.

Slowly, I climbed the stone stair. I prayed that whoever had run past me was gone. I hoped no-one was waiting at the top. Above all, I wondered what was going on.

Somehow, I made it back across the meadow and through the kitchen garden. I was as tense and alert as the small creature hiding from the owl. At any moment, I expected the unknown figure to appear.

I reached for the door handle at the front of the house. A hand gripped my arm and I screamed in shock. My scream was muffled by another hand over my mouth. I struggled violently. There was a muttered curse.

'Hold still, dammit. Be silent.'

I recognised the growling, deep voice. It was Charles, Viscount Bowerly. Immediately, I calmed. I did not imagine he intended me harm.

'Please unhand me,' I whispered severely.

The hands across my mouth and arm dropped. He stood close, and I was too aware of his height and breadth. I was conscious of my state of undress. At least it was dark. Hopefully he couldn't see the trailing skirts of my nightgown or the state of my hair, loosened as it was from its plait.

There was a long pause.

His scent was of male sweat, leather and horse. Had he been out riding at night? Was it his horse's hooves I had heard earlier? Before I could form questions of my own, he was interrogating me.

'Why are you here?'

I could ask the same of you. I did not voice my thought. As I framed a careful reply, he spoke again impatiently.

'What are you doing outside the Hall? Speak up, Miss Thorne. Now.'

'I heard a noise.'

'A noise?' He seemed to relax slightly. Yet still he stood too close. Close enough that I felt the heat of his body, and a strange heightened awareness of how his hands had felt upon me … I shook away this whim.

'Yes, I think maybe a horse's hooves. It

was foolish of me to venture out. It must have been your horse I heard.'

He frowned. I barely made out his features in the moonlight.

'It isn't safe to wander out here at night. You must return to your rooms. I shall escort you inside.'

'There is no need for that, my lord. I am quite capable of finding my way alone.'

He grunted. I took this as agreement and turned away from him. My pulse was beating quickly. I felt his gaze upon me, burning into my back. I didn't look behind me. Once I was safely in my bedroom, I listened at the door. There was silence. Charles had not entered the house after me. Where, then, was he going? Where had he been?

I mulled over our brief conversation. My first impression of him had not changed. He unsettled me. I realised he had not confirmed or denied that he had been out riding. He had cleverly kept his focus on my whereabouts. And if the viscount had indeed been out, where had he been?

I sat down rather heavily as another thought struck me. Was it possible that he was the man who had carried the lantern to the beach? Had he hit me hard as he ran past me on the cliff path?

4

A few days later, Mary and I went to visit Sarah and Charlotte. The vicarage was a pleasant rambling house built of grey Yorkshire stone. Sarah looked pleased to see us as she welcomed us inside. The interior reminded me sharply of Chelmley Wood. My throat constricted, and it was a moment before I could speak. The rooms were of shabby elegance and there were books everywhere. The atmosphere evoked my dear father. My sense of loss was intense. It took Sarah's gentle guiding hand to bring me back to the present day.

'Will you take a seat, Amelia? I'll call for tea. Charlotte, you may take Mary with you to the nursery and show her your toys.'

'Thank you.' I managed a smile.

'Are you alright?' Sarah asked. 'You're rather pale.'

'I'm fine, really. It's just that your home

reminds me of mine. Or, rather, my old home where I grew up.'

'And these are sad memories?'

'No, they're all happy — but I miss it, and I miss my dear departed father. Forgive me, Sarah, I have no wish to bring a gloominess to your day.'

'Not at all,' she said. 'I completely understand. I'm so sorry you lost your father. I suppose that is why you are now a governess.'

I nodded. 'Yes, my circumstances were such that there was no alternative. I had to find work. I've been very lucky to find a place at Bowerly Hall.'

'Still, it's hard work looking after a lively child. I love my little sister with all my heart, but she exhausts me some days.'

'Charlotte's your sister?' I asked in surprise.

'Yes, of course ... why, did you think she was mine?' Sarah laughed.

I blushed. That was exactly what I had thought. It hadn't occurred to me that Sarah might still be unwed at her age. Thinking about it now, it made perfect sense. She had told me she cared for her father at the vicarage. She had made no mention of caring for a husband too.

'There is a large age gap between Charlotte and me,' Sarah said. 'My poor mother had eight children, but Charlotte and I are the only survivors.'

'I'm sorry, I didn't mean to pry,' I told her.

'Please don't apologise! I should have introduced us properly that day at the meadow. Any misunderstanding is entirely my fault.' She smiled mischievously. 'You really think I'm old enough to be mother to an eight-year-old?'

'Oh!' My fingers flew to cover my mouth. How rude of me. Sarah could barely be more than twenty-two, like myself.

'I'm teasing you, Amelia; it's quite alright. I'm flattered you think I'd make a good mother. I hope very much one day to be one when I do get married.'

'Are you....do you have someone in mind?' I seemed incapable of making polite conversation.

Sarah took it in her stride. She was very relaxed, and I realised that we were chatting like old friends, rather than two young women who barely knew each other. I felt myself slowly relax, too.

She flushed prettily at my question. 'My father has a curate, a Mr James Smith … He is a very kind and gentle man.'

'You have feelings for him?'

'There is no understanding of that nature between us,' she said quickly. 'But, yes, I hold him in very high regard.'

The prettiness of her features, all lit up as she described him, made me think he was a lucky man. I hoped there would be a happy future for them.

'What about you?' Sarah asked. 'Is there anyone special?'

'Not at all,' I said, with a rueful smile. 'My father and I led a quiet life at Chelmley Wood, and we didn't have many visitors. It wasn't possible to make the acquaintance of any young men. If I had gone to London, it might have been different — but that didn't happen. Anyway, I don't regret it. I enjoyed being with my father and roaming the countryside. I suppose, if I'd had a husband, he might have forbidden me my freedom.'

'That depends very much on the husband one chooses,' Sarah said tartly.

For some reason, an image of Viscount Bowerly flashed before me. His dark, brooding good looks and piercing blue eyes. What kind of husband had he been? It wouldn't have surprised me if he'd kept his wife imprisoned in a tower. He was a mysterious, dangerous sort of man.

The tea and cakes had arrived, and Sarah busied herself pouring the liquid into delicate teacups and offering a plate of small cream fancies.

'How do you like Bowerly Hall?' she asked, once we both had food and drink. 'Lady Anne is lovely, don't you find?'

'I am beginning to find my feet at the Hall,' I said. 'Lady Anne has made me most welcome. Not everyone is quite so pleasant.'

She raised her eyebrows in surprise, and I told her about Mrs Dane and Mrs Bell; but made sure also to say how friendly Peggy was.

'I know Mrs Bell,' Sarah said. 'You'd do well to keep out of her way. Her husband is a nasty piece of work. He's well-known in the village for his hasty fists after a few drinks. My father has visited several times over the years to talk to the man after some altercation or other.'

A shiver ran up my spine. It was horrible to think that the woman who hated me on sight had a violent husband.

'Do you know her cousin, Mrs Smith? She was Mary's nanny before I arrived.'

Sarah shook her head. 'Is that Aggie Smith? I do recollect my father talking about her. She was often at the Bells' cottage, he said. I never met her. Why do you ask?'

'It doesn't matter,' I said. I didn't know Sarah well enough to share with her my suspicions of Mrs Smith's unkindness to Mary.

'What of Lord Charles? Have you seen much of him?' Sarah asked curiously.

I could hardly tell her of my encounter with him late at night. I hadn't really come to any conclusions about it. In fact, if I thought about the three times in total that I'd met him so far, he hadn't on any of these occasions put himself out to be pleasant!

'It's so sad that his wife died,' Sarah went on. 'Miss Mary was just a tiny baby. He was very much in love with Lady Catherine, and it was such a shock to all of us when she caught a fever and died. I remember the baby was whisked away to London to her mother's family for a while, for fear she'd get ill. We never saw the Viscount after that; not for years. They said he'd gone abroad to grieve for her. He's only been back in the country since last spring.'

'How tragic for all of them. Imagine how Lady Anne must have felt! She lost her son, her daughter-in-law, and her grandchild, all in one swoop.'

'I never thought of it like that,' Sarah agreed. 'It was awful for them. Miss Mary came back once the threat of fever had gone. So I suppose Lady Anne at least had some comfort in that.'

'What was she like? Lady Catherine, I mean?' I couldn't help asking.

'She was beautiful. She had glorious blonde curls and big brown eyes. They say she was the belle of all the balls the year she came out. She took one look at Viscount Bowerly and she'd have no other. She pursued him until he fell head over heels in love with her, and he brought her back to Bowerly.'

'Which is quite a contrast to the lively social bustle of London,' I remarked.

'Yes, but she took to it like the proverbial duck to water,' Sarah said eagerly. 'She loved her gardens, and she brought six gardeners back from Paris to tend to the grounds. The flowers were gorgeous. It's a pity you couldn't have seen the place back then.'

I was beginning to regret the turn of our conversation that I had wrought. What had I wanted to hear? That Charles' wife was ugly, or that he didn't love her? That she'd made him unhappy at Bowerly? What on earth was the matter with me? I hid my disappointment and castigated myself for uncharitable thoughts.

'Was he always so short-tempered? Or did he change after his wife's death?' I asked.

'Short-tempered? Is he really? I'm afraid I don't know him very well. We hardly move in the same social circles. He and Lady Anne do come to the village festival, but apart from that, we don't mix.'

'Lady Anne did say they will be spending the summers in London,' I remembered.

'She certainly spent last summer in London, but of course he was away before that, so I suppose they will both go from now on. It will be quiet for you.'

'I don't mind. Besides, there are autumn, winter and spring to be experienced first. I'm sure it will all be rather different from the south coast. I'm not looking forward to the freezing snow.'

'It isn't so bad!' Sarah laughed. 'You'll get used to it.'

At that moment came the sound of

hearty male voices and the next two men arrived in the room bringing a blast of cold air with them. Sarah rose to greet them and turned then to me with a smile.

'Amelia, let me introduce my father and Mr James Smith.'

'Don't get up, my dear,' the vicar said kindly, clasping my hand with his own large warm one. 'I'm very glad to find that Sarah has company. She spends far too much time on her own.'

I liked Sarah's father immediately. He was a large man, with tufts of grey hair and a ruddy complexion, and the air of someone completely content with their lot in life. My attention switched to his companion, who politely shook my hand. This was Sarah's young man — or perhaps not quite yet. He was well-built, not tall but stocky, and although not handsome to my eye, I could see why Sarah would describe him as gentle and kind. His features were mild and pleasant.

The vicar was shaking his head. 'It's a terrible business. It really is.'

'What has happened, Father?'

'Another burglary. This time at Fonteyne Abbey. They've lost gold candlesticks, linen, and family porcelain. It's not as if they have too much of great value. I wonder why the blackguard chose them.'

'Perhaps because they were an easy target,' James Smith said. 'The old lady lives there quite alone except for the servants, does she not?'

And I saw that there was more to Sarah's James than at first met the eye. A keen intelligence lay behind his mild manner. Sarah's eyes twinkled with pride as the vicar patted the younger man on the shoulder.

'Indeed, I should have thought of that myself. How very true.'

'Which makes the perpetrator a coward as well as evil,' I said indignantly.

Although I had never met the old lady at the Abbey, I sympathised with the horrible event she'd been through. How awful to be so vulnerable to a thief! I was thankful that Bowerly was home to so many people. Surely we would not be a target?

'It's so frightening,' Sarah murmured with a shiver.

At once, James moved a little closer to her, as if he would protect her. 'You must have no fear, Sarah,' he said earnestly. 'Your father and I will let no harm come to you or the vicarage.'

'Especially as we have no riches for a thief to steal,' her father added with a booming laugh. It broke the sombre mood that had surrounded us.

'When did the spate of break-ins begin?' I asked curiously.

The vicar thought for a moment, a frown wrinkling his forehead. 'Let me see … I believe it has been a year already. Goodness, how time does fly. Yes, a twelvemonth.'

'But the thefts are not regular,' James said; slowly, as if thinking it out. 'Not one a month, or some such thing. They are sporadic. At first there were long gaps between them. Now, there has been a cluster recently — as if he's gaining confidence.'

'Or desperation,' Sarah suggested.

'Maybe he needs more money now than he did before.'

I remembered what Sarah had told me. That the Viscount Bowerly had only been back in the country a little more than a year. Was it coincidence? I said nothing of this, however. I felt that my companions might be shocked at my train of thought.

But then I wondered why he would be the thief. Surely he had no need to steal other people's belongings? Bowerly Hall looked to be prosperous. Unless he had debts ... It was possible. Yet what proof did I have except that he had acted strangely? None. It was all in my imagination.

My head began to ache, and soon I made my excuses to Sarah, gathered up Mary from the playroom, and made my way back to the Hall. I was being foolish. I must put such musings out of my head, I decided.

Mary was tired from playing with Charlotte, and lay down for a nap. I left Peggy in charge of her and went downstairs. I wondered how to fill my afternoon. I could hardly join the servants: I wasn't ready for another of Mrs Dane's chilly stares, or a snappy comment from Mrs Bell. Instead, I found my footsteps taking me to the far side of the house, and to the stables.

I loved horses. I often rode at Chelmley Wood, and knew most of the countryside around it from the back of my beloved Betsey. The stables at Bowerly Hall were much larger than those at Chelmley, and I remembered Lady Anne saying that her son bred fine horses on the estate.

I stroked the nose of one handsome black beast over the stable door. He snickered in a friendly fashion. I breathed in the scent of horses, hay and feed. A couple of stable hands looked at me as they went about their work but didn't speak.

'His name is Raven.'

The voice came from behind me and I started. I turned to find Charles watching me. My heartbeat quickened. He walked over to join me.

'He is a beauty,' I said.

'He is of impeccable lineage.'

I was inexplicably disappointed with Charles. Was that all that mattered? I supposed so, if breeding horses was a business. Personally, I cared more for the personality, the spirit of a horse. Betsey had been a gentle ride with a sweet nature. Raven certainly looked regal, but not too fierce. Unlike his master.

Then Charles smiled. It swept away his brooding expression. It made his blue gaze lighten like summer seas. My heart lurched.

'Not only that,' he said, stroking Raven's nose in exactly the spot I had, 'he never loses his temper with me. And that is a rare quality.'

'Do you often bring others' wrath upon you?' I asked mildly.

'I have a knack for it, it's true.'

'How awful for you.' I heard the teasing in my own voice, and it struck me that we were bantering with each other. I was seeing a different side to the Viscount.

'Do you enjoy riding, Miss Thorne?'

'Oh yes,' I said enthusiastically, until I remembered where I was. 'At least, I used to. At home.'

'Where, might I ask, is home?'

I flushed and shook my head. 'Of course, my home is here now. I'm sorry. I didn't mean to …'

'Come, Miss Thorne, I asked you a question. You must answer it.'

I glanced up at him uncertainly. His expression was not unkind despite the order he'd given. Indeed it looked as if he genuinely waited to hear my answer.

I took in a deep breath. 'My home was at Chelmley Wood, in the South Downs. You won't know of it, of course, but it was a lovely, special place.'

'I do know of it. In fact I have fond memories of the place.'

'You do?' Surprise made me squeak.

His smile widened. 'A small river runs through the grounds, does it not? A great orchard backs the house, and I seem to recall my partiality to coconut biscuits being indulged by the cook, although I cannot bring her name to mind.'

'Mrs Gilmour,' I whispered. A small pain twisted in my chest. I swallowed down the sudden ache to be back there, not only in the physical space but in the past. A past where father and Mrs Gilmour still ruled the house with love and a guiding hand between them.

'Ah yes, that's it. The indomitable Mrs Gilmour. I have never since tasted such wonderful biscuits.'

'Why were you visiting?' I asked. I tried and failed to find a memory of him in my past.

'My father was very interested in geology. I believe your father had the best library in England on the subject, and he was duly invited to come and study the books. I was very young, but he took me with him. What excitement for a small boy! It was an adventure.'

If he had been a small boy then, I must have been only a baby or toddler. Which explained why I didn't remember him. How odd, that now we had a connection of sorts. It felt rather … *good*. I reminded myself that I didn't trust him. Though he was good with animals — Raven was clearly besotted with him. They say that animals can tell if someone is to be trusted. But still, I was cautious.

A bell rang somewhere distantly in the Hall. Charles stiffened, and all at once his smile vanished to be replaced with the darkness I had come to expect. It was in his black brows and changing blue eyes and a scowl that set his jaw too tight. What a pity it was his usual way. I much preferred the smiling man of a few minutes before. The Charles of orchards, rivers and sweet coconut biscuits. The man who whispered comfort to his horse. Who spared time to talk to his daughter's governess and attempt to calm her homesickness.

He bowed and made to take his leave. Just before he rounded the end of the stables, he stopped.

'You must borrow a horse and go riding, if you will. Whenever you wish to, ask the stable hands and they will find what you need.'

With that, he was gone. I was left with Raven, a smile lingering on my lips at his generous offer.

5

The invitation to dinner came as I was reading a story to Mary in the nursery before she ate that evening. Mrs Dane's pursed lips indicated her displeasure. I was sure she wanted me to refuse. Part of me wished to. But another part of me was too intrigued to say no. I nodded my thanks gracefully. She swept away on bristling skirts.

What was I to wear? Eventually I chose my green silk dress. It accentuated my waist and the skirt flowed prettily over the petticoats. I liked the neat sleeves and the cool whisper of the material on my wrists. At my neck I wore my mother's pendant as always. It gave me courage. For I was apprehensive, I admit.

Who had given the invitation? Was it Lady Anne? Did she wish to speak to me further about my mother and their childhood days? In which case, would her son disapprove of having the governess at their dining table? Or was it Charles who had invited me? Perhaps our conversation earlier had inclined him well towards me. Or maybe he pitied me. I hoped not. I did not want to eat with them out of charity. If Charles had initiated the invitation, was I then to be faced with Lady Anne's annoyance? Questions, too many questions. I sighed. There were to be no answers until I made my way downstairs to dine.

I need not have worried. Both Lady Anne and Charles greeted me pleasantly. They were dressed formally, and I was glad of my green gown's elegance. I might be lower than my hosts on the social scale, but tonight, no-one watching would have been able to tell.

The dining room was invitingly warm. A fire crackled in the enormous hearth and the table was lit with candles. The yellow candlelight glinted off the crystalware and silver cutlery. There was a beautiful arrangement of pink and red roses as a centrepiece, and I caught their sweet scent as I took my place.

'You look very charming tonight, Miss Thorne,' Charles said politely.

'Doesn't she just,' chimed in Lady Anne with a smile. 'That wonderful shade of green is perfect for your hair.'

I felt Charles' gaze flicker briefly to my head and felt strangely self-conscious. A little heat rose in my skin. I wasn't sure what to say. Thankfully, I was spared answering. At that moment, the door crashed open and a young man entered.

Startled, we all looked to him. I had the oddest sensation that I had met him before. Immediately, I realised why. He was the image of the Viscount. But not quite. As I studied him further, I saw that he had Charles' dark brown hair and black brows. Even the patrician nose. Yet these features failed to create the same handsome face. The strong jaw was lacking. This man had a slightly receding chin, and a flabbiness to his cheeks which spoke of indulgence.

'Francis!' Lady Anne cried happily and went to embrace him.

I glanced over at the Viscount. His face

was shadowed. Clearly he did not share his mother's pleasure in their guest.

'This is most unexpected, and most welcome,' Lady Anne trilled, guiding the newcomer by hooking her elbow into his and bringing him to the table.

I was unsettled to look up and find him watching me.

'And who is this, dear Aunt?' he said. 'You must introduce me this instant.'

'Francis, this is Miss Amelia Thorne, governess to little Mary and the daughter of a friend of mine. Amelia, this is my nephew Francis Williams. How lovely of you to visit, you should have warned us you were coming.'

'And spoil the surprise? Never!' he teased her, and slid into the chair next to mine. 'I am delighted to make your acquaintance, Miss Thorne — or may I call you Amelia?'

'You may not, Francis,' Charles cut in sharply. 'It would hardly be proper, since you don't know Miss Thorne.' His face was hawklike and if I had been his cousin Francis, I'd have been shaking in my highly polished boots.

Francis took little heed. He pressed rather close to me as if to share a secret. I saw the pores in his skin and smelt brandy fumes on his breath.

'Charles always liked to be the boss of me,' he whispered loudly. 'Even when we were boys together.'

'I seem to remember that you needed a firm hand,' his cousin said. 'It was my duty as the elder to look after you.'

Mrs Bidens' words came back to me. She'd described Charles as a solemn boy.

'Ah well,' Francis said, leaning back on his chair, very much the lord and master. 'What delights are for dinner, Aunt? I am desperately hungry, even if it's bad manners to say so.'

He had a boyish charm, a mischievous way that contrasted to his cousin's stoniness. It was hard not to find it appealing. He winked at me. I found myself warming to his charm. What was Charles' problem? He sat at the head of the table glowering.

'If you didn't play the cards so often, you'd be able to afford a decent dinner at your own home,' he said.

Francis put up his palms in mock despair. 'I don't have the wonderful Mrs Bell cooking for me. My own cook provides stew after stew. I desire variety.' His lazy smile included us all in his little joke.

Lady Anne looked pleased. 'No stews tonight, you'll be glad to hear, then. I believe we are having chicken dishes. Seriously, my dear, how are you? We haven't had the pleasure of your company for weeks.'

He waved a vague hand in the air. 'My dear Aunt, I have been busy with various ventures. Tonight, however, you have all my attention.' His eyes met mine and it was hard to look away.

When I did so, Charles was frowning at me. *Well, really!* I thought. Was he annoyed at me now? I was doing nothing wrong. I determined there and then to enjoy my evening. If that meant being entertained by Francis, then that was fine and good. I would not be put out by my host's stony expression.

The footmen brought in the first course: a thin consommé soup which was very tasty. I sipped at it slowly, wanting to linger over dinner. A meal that, for once, I wasn't eating alone in my rooms. Instead there were voices chatting, the clink of cutlery and the sound of wine being poured into crystal glasses. The room was neither too cold nor too warm. I was aware of all my senses absorbing the moment like a thirsty person in a desert craving water.

'Your accent suggests you are not from these parts, Miss Thorne,' Francis said.

'I am from the south coast,' I replied, conscious of the blue stare from my left at the head of the table.

'You must find our rough Yorkshire climate a shock.'

'I find it a little cold,' I said, 'but I'm sure I shall soon adapt to it.'

'What a terrible time to arrive,' he said. 'You have the cold months ahead of you. You must be sure to wrap up warmly.' I felt his gaze on my skin above the neckline of my dress. Suddenly, it was uncomfortable. I was conscious that my neckline dipped, and I wished I had tucked a ruche of linen into it. Almost as I thought that, he focused on cutting the chicken on his plate — the next course had silently arrived. Perhaps I had imagined my discomfort.

'Miss Thorne is a horse woman,' Charles said suddenly.

'Indeed, how wonderful,' Francis said. 'You must come and visit my humble abode. I keep a good stable. You would be impressed.'

'I am certainly impressed with the stables here,' I said. 'I'm looking forward to riding again; I've missed it so.' I was wittering. My nerves were on edge, and I always spoke too freely when tense.

'We can't have you missing the horses!' Francis cried, all bonhomie. 'Goodness, no. You must promise me to visit. I have a charming mare that is just right for you.'

I was conscious of all my companions, even while I met no-one's direct gaze. Charles, to my left, seemingly stilled for my response. Lady Anne opposite, smiling fondly at her nephew's kindness. Francis to my right, so close I felt the heat from him, and a slight sourness of body odour. His stare seemed to assess me. If I enjoyed horse-riding, then I must be a gentlewoman of some sort. He was mentally placing me in a hierarchy: of that, I was suddenly sure. I didn't like it. Clearly, whatever he'd decided, I was worthy of an invitation to his stables. I decided immediately that I had no wish to go there, however gallant or amusing a companion he had made himself out to be.

'Come, what do you say?' he urged me.

I carefully laid down my silver knife and fork amongst the ruins of the chicken on my plate. The footmen glided silently into the room and removed the course. It allowed me a moment to gather my wits. I didn't wish to appear ungrateful. Equally, for no reason I could lay a finger on, I had no desire to spend time alone with Francis Williams.

Dessert was brought. A bright pink posset of rhubarb, an almond cake and preserved cherries in a dish. I took a little of each, and saw Charles' mouth quirk in amusement. I wasn't really hungry after the delicious chicken dishes, but I was tempted by sweet flavours. Mrs Bell might not be a very nice person but she could most definitely cook.

Beside me, Francis gave a tiny cough, for attention. *Like a small boy*, I thought with humour.

'It is very kind of you to invite me,' I said. 'But I have promised His Lordship to accept the offer of a horse from the stables here first.'

The two men locked stares briefly. Francis was the first to look away. With a small sulky curl to his lip, he cut a wedge of cake without offering it to anyone else. A couple of gulps and the slice had disappeared.

Lady Anne filled the uncomfortable silence that had descended on the company.

'How is your mother? Does her health improve?'

'My mother's lungs are in fine fettle. She complains like stink about everything.

As for the rest of her, there is no change. She lies abed each day and has all the servants running around her.' There was no mistaking the sulkiness in his tone now.

Lady Anne looked rather shocked. 'Francis, please, show charity. Your poor mother ... my sister-in-law is not a well person. We must surely find it in our hearts to show compassion.'

'You're right. I am contrite. It is only that there is no peace in my home. I swear, at times it's as if she hates me ...'

'Your imagination runs riot,' Lady Anne said sternly. 'Come, there must be no more of this sort of talk.'

Francis leapt up from the table. He smiled widely but it did not reach his eyes. It fooled his aunt, though. She smiled back, obviously relieved his mood was over.

'Will you forgive me if I go downstairs to see Mrs Bell?' he asked.

'Oh, well ... is that entirely ...'

He bestowed another golden smile upon her. 'You know how fond I am of your cook. I must have spent more childhood days here than at my own home.'

Lady Anne nodded. 'Yes, yes, I suppose that's right. Well, I can see no harm in it. Charles?'

Charles shrugged. 'It matters not to me. Francis must do as he sees fit. As he inevitably does.'

There was a veiled message there; but for the life of me, I could not tell what it was. Whatever barb was intended, it hit its target. Francis flushed darkly. He offered a quick bow to me and left the room.

The meal came to an end quite soon after Francis' departure. The mood had changed. Lady Anne was agitated and spilled her glass of wine. Charles finished his dessert in silence. I thought how self-contained he was. He obviously felt no compunction to make chit-chat even out of politeness' sake. I finished my desserts and then made my excuses. I thanked my host and hostess for the pleasure of joining them at dinner. It was no lie. I had enjoyed myself. I hoped there might be other such evenings in future.

I took a candle to light me to my rooms. The hall was dark. Perhaps the footmen had forgotten to light the sconces. Whatever the reason, the space was dim with dark shadows in the corners. My heart clenched. I was fearful, but I wasn't sure why. Just a sense of something not quite right. A sensation of being watched. The skin on the back of my neck prickled.

I was about to go upstairs when I heard voices. They were low and muttered. It was the furtive edge to them that made me hesitate. I tiptoed gently over to where the servants' staircase descended. I couldn't see anyone from that angle. It was late, but of course the maids and other staff worked long days. There was all the clearing-up of our dinner crockery to do. Besides, Francis was down there visiting Mrs Bell. I knew I should go upstairs.

Instead, my feet took me slowly down. I decided that, if I was challenged, I'd say I was visiting Peggy. I didn't particularly want to see Francis Williams again, and hoped he was busy charming Mrs Bell in the kitchen.

A footman rushed past me with a murmured apology. He held a stack of dishes. The butler was instructing another footman. He didn't look at me as I went past. I tried to think where the voices had come from. There was a small extra pantry off the main kitchen. The kitchen itself was empty. That surprised me. Where was Mrs Bell?

She came out from the small pantry. I ducked out of the kitchen and pressed against the far wall of the staircase. Francis followed her out. I couldn't make out what they were saying. There was too much noise from the maids in the rooms beyond. Francis looked annoyed. Mrs Bell was shaking her head. Then he spoke briefly. Whatever he said, it had an effect. The cook froze, then nodded. Her round, ruddy face was unhappy.

What was going on? It didn't look like a fond reunion between the cook and her employer's nephew. I was stuck in the dark corner between the stairs and the wall. I waited until Francis left. Mrs Bell went back into the kitchen. Her broad back was rigid. I heard her shout at the maids. Whatever Francis had said, she was as angry as he had seemed.

I went softly upstairs, meeting no-one. I put my candle carefully beside my bed. The fire was out in the hearth. It was banked up for the morning. The grey ashes smelt acrid. I undressed quickly, as it was cold in the room. I blew out my candle and pulled the covers over me.

As I lay there, trying to sleep, images of the evening flooded my mind. The good meal that Mrs Bell had provided. The beautiful room with its decorations and golden light. Francis's unexpected arrival as a guest. Charles' disapproval of his cousin, which was so obvious. Lady Anne's fondness for her nephew … Something nagged at the back of my head: a thought so thin it was like the early-morning mist. I tried to grasp it, to make it solid, but couldn't.

There was a creaking noise outside my door. I sat up in bed, all hope of sleep gone. My senses were sharp. I waited. After a long moment in which I believed I'd imagined the noise, it came again. Then footsteps receding. Someone had walked up to my door, listened at it, and then gone away.

I stayed sitting up for a long while, until I was certain there was no-one outside. I watched the door handle, barely visible in the ray of moonlight coming from the window. What horror if it should suddenly move! But it didn't.

Who had listened at the door? And why?

Eventually, I sank back onto my pillows, exhausted. I couldn't stay awake. As sleep claimed me, the wispy thought condensed. It was about Lady Anne. After Francis had left to see Mrs Bell, she'd been tense. So agitated, in fact, that she'd spilled her glass of wine. Why was she so nervous?

6

'I'm hungry. Why hasn't Peggy brought my breakfast?' Mary asked, pressing her fingers to her stomach.

'I don't know,' I said. 'She is rather late today. Perhaps it is busy in the kitchen.'

Peggy pushed open the door to the nursery, and Mary clapped her hands. The odour of boiled egg and hot buttered toast was enticing.

'Sorry,' Peggy said, 'I'm rushed off me feet today.'

There were dark circles under her eyes, and her freckles were brown against her white face. Her hair was more unruly than ever, as if she hadn't had time to place her cap on properly.

'Are you alright?' I asked.

'I'm okay. It's Edna and Lil, the kitchen maids. They're not well at all. Both of the footmen's got it and all. Mrs Dane's rushed off her feet. Now Mrs Bell's complaining of a sore head. The breakfasts aren't ready and there's no-one to serve it up.'

'What illness have they got?' I had some small experience of nursing my father through various ailments. Maybe I could be of use.

'It's a fever, a bad one,' Peggy said, shaking her head.

'Has the doctor been called?'

'He's just been. He's left instructions on what to do for the patients. Not much, in my opinion. Just keep them cool till the fever breaks. Plenty to drink and lots of rest until they're better. You should've seen Mrs Dane's face when he said about the resting!' Peggy managed a laugh. 'She's none too happy to see her maids lying in bed.'

'Oh, dear. I must go and speak with Mrs Dane,' I said firmly. 'Mary, after breakfast, you are invited to visit with your grandmamma for a little while. I will fetch you for your luncheon.'

Mary brightened. She loved spending time with Lady Anne. She also loved her food. The mention of both grandmother and luncheon all at once made her smile wide. I noticed the healthy pink tinge to her skin, and thought she had put on some weight, to her advantage. I was glad she would be kept occupied all morning. I had things to do.

'How exactly can you help?' Mrs Dane asked stiffly.

It was too much to expect that she'd welcome me warmly. I took a breath in and tried again.

'Peggy has explained that there's a fever going round the staff. I'm offering to help look after them. Miss Mary is with Lady Anne, and I am free for a few hours. Let me tend to Edna and Lil. That way, you can pursue your other tasks.'

She pursed her lips as if she'd refuse, and looked at me suspiciously. I bit back a sharp comment. It was as if she thought I had an ulterior motive. Then, to my relief, she nodded.

'Very well. You may nurse the maids. If they show signs of improving, please send them downstairs. I am extremely short-staffed.'

Once I had reached Edna and Lil in their small attic bedroom, I knew they were not going to be going downstairs for a while. They tossed and turned, moaning. Their faces were shiny with sweat, and the room stank of it. I opened the window slightly to let in fresh air. I didn't want them to get too cold, yet it was vital that I bring down their temperature.

It was a long morning of carrying bowls of water up, and taking soiled water down. The two maids were no better, and I heard from Peggy that one of the stable hands was sick now too. I made very sure that I scrubbed my face and hands well before I joined Mary for lunch.

She was sitting, kicking her heels on her chair and reading a book. I frowned and she stopped her kicking.

'That's better,' I said approvingly. 'Did you enjoy your morning?'

She nodded. 'Yes, Grandmamma told me stories and showed me her new tea set. It's got pink roses on it and gold paint on the rims. She's going to give it to me when I'm a grown lady.'

'Well, what's the matter, then?' I asked, seeing that she wasn't in the best of moods.

'I was meant to stay until luncheon, wasn't I? But Grandmamma sent me away early because her head was sore. Did I do something wrong?'

'No, of course not,' I said, gathering her to me for a cuddle. 'When someone has a headache, they need to be quiet and lie down.'

I prayed that Lady Anne was not succumbing to the fever.

'When am I going to get my food? Why isn't Peggy here?'

'Peggy's very busy today. You stay here, and I'll go and fetch our luncheon from the kitchen.'

The kitchen was unusually quiet. Mrs Bell was stirring a large pot of steaming soup. She rubbed her forehead wearily and glanced up at my footsteps.

'What do you want?' she said rudely.

'Miss Mary is hungry. I've come to

fetch us something to eat.'

'There's soup and bread, that's all. I'm on me own today; there's no-one else to help with the cooking and preparing and chopping and whatnot.'

'Where's Peggy?'

She snorted and made a sour face. 'How would I know? Mrs Dane's gone and taken her for other chores. Cleaning upstairs, I should imagine.'

Poor Peggy. The other maids' sickness meant extra duties for her. I hoped she wouldn't get sick too.

'You'll have to help yourself. There's a ladle there. Plates on the rack. Cutlery in that drawer.' Her tone was barely civil.

I felt like snapping back at her. It wasn't my fault that I'd been hired in place of her cousin. She shouldn't hold a grudge against me. Then I remembered Sarah's warning about Mrs Bell's husband. It was best that I didn't engage too much with the woman. Unlike her, I could be polite.

'Thank you so much,' I said calmly.

She looked briefly surprised, then narrowed her eyes. She couldn't fault me for manners — even if she suspected I was being ever so slightly sarcastic. Without further ado, I took hold of the enormous, heavy ladle, and managed to fill two plates of vegetable soup. There was a wheaten loaf on a board. I took up the knife that lay beside it, and cut two slices. They were uneven, but would be tasty nonetheless. I saw a silver tray and took it to place the food on. Out of the corner of my eye, I saw Mrs Bell open her mouth to protest, but she said nothing. I realised that the tray was for the use of the butler. It was too late, though: I'd already filled it, and wasn't going to take everything off to search for a different one. If Mrs Bell wanted to help, then good. If not, she had to take the consequences. With that tart notion, I lifted the tray and walked out of her kitchen.

'It's like an indoor picnic,' I explained to Mary, 'that's why it's just soup and bread.'

'No cake?' she asked dubiously.

I'd forgotten to ask Mrs Bell for a pudding. I didn't feel like venturing back to the kitchen.

'No cake, unfortunately. Still, this will fill us up nicely. Now, be a good girl and begin.'

There was a knock at the door.

'Come in,' I called, thinking it was Peggy.

Mrs Dane entered, her black dress rustling with starch.

I stood up. 'Mrs Dane, is everything alright? Is there more sickness in the house? Can I help you?'

She smiled. She actually smiled! 'You've been a big help to me already, Miss Thorne. I think I may have misjudged you. I hope you will accept my thanks for your work today. Peggy tells me that Edna and Lil are much calmer than this morning. All down to your care, I'm sure.'

It was the longest speech I'd heard her make. My heart lightened. I smiled back at her.

'Not at all. It was my pleasure. I'm glad to hear the maids are improving. Although I'd caution against them getting up too soon.'

'Have no worry; I am quite aware they need to recuperate. The doctor made that clear. It looks like we will have to hold the fort for a few days to come.'

It warmed me to hear myself included. 'I'm sure we can hold the fort admirably, Mrs Dane. I look forward to it.'

'Good.' She was all business once more, as if embarrassed at her loose tongue. But I sensed the change in her. We were perhaps not friends yet, but possibly allies or acquaintances. On the same side, at the very least.

'I will look in on Edna and Lil before I go to bed tonight,' I said, 'and if there is anything else you need me to do, please let me know.'

'Very well. I'll leave you to your charge now. I know you will be busy until the evening.' She swept out of the room.

Mary and I exchanged a glance.

'She likes you now,' the little girl said happily.

'That is a step in the right direction. Now, let us finish up, and you can take a short nap before we learn some French.'

I needed some fresh air. While Mary slept, I went to the stables. As I neared the corner, there came the sound of galloping hooves and loud voices. A horse and rider narrowly missed me as they streaked across the cobblestones and out of the gates. The air had been forced from my lungs. It took me a moment to steady myself. If I hadn't moved swiftly, I might have been knocked to the ground. Who was the heedless rider?

'Are you quite alright, Miss Thorne?' Charles' deep voice came from behind me.

'Yes, but no thanks to your visitor,' I replied without thinking.

'My cousin's manners are not what they should be.'

So it was Francis Williams who had so carelessly ridden through the stables. In a temper, it would seem. What had the two men argued about? It was not my place to ask. There was little love between Charles and Francis, that was clear to any observer. The air at dinner the night before had quite bristled at times.

'I'm taking a short ride through the estate,' Charles said. 'Will you join me?'

I was surprised and pleased. It would be lovely to ride out. And Charles, despite his quiet ways, would be a good companion, I decided. There was just one problem.

'I have left Mary having a nap upstairs. I shouldn't be away too long.'

'We won't be more than a half-hour,' he said. 'I have business to attend to at the house. Mary will not notice you gone, I assure you.'

This was her father speaking. If he was happy for me to leave her, then I should not worry. Besides, Peggy was working on the third storey, dusting furniture and cleaning the fire grates. If Mary did wake and call, Peggy would go to her. With my mind settled, I looked forward to riding out.

'Come, we will find you a suitable mount,' Charles said.

Raven was already saddled, and a groom held his reins. The big black horse whinnied and stamped his hooves impatiently. Charles stroked his velvet nose.

'A moment, and you shall have your freedom.'

Another stable hand brought out a pretty mare, soft brown like caramel, with a white streak down her forehead.

'This is Grace. She is gentle, and not prone to heading her own way. Does she suit you?'

It was gratifying to be asked my opinion. I nodded my approval.

'I must change. I can hardly ride in this outfit.' I hesitated. If Charles was in a hurry, would he wait for me?

'Yes, of course. I will meet you here. The horses will be ready.' He inclined his head. I rushed happily back to the house to dress appropriately.

A short while later, I grasped at Grace's saddle with excitement. My riding habit was old but perfectly respectable, and I was glad I had brought it with me from my uncle's house. Once up on Grace's placid back, I was content. I too wanted my freedom, and riding was the way to get it.

We trotted out of the gates and onto the fields. The landscape was all rough green grass, thick hawthorn hedges and sturdy oaks at the margins. The leaves were turning brown. A late-season skylark trilled and soared. Above us, a flock of plovers flew over. Their black and white colours were stark against the blue sky. The air was cold and sharp. Grace's breath steamed out. I smelt oiled leather, the sweet odour of horse and a hint of gorse blooms.

'Ready?' Charles called. He kicked at Raven's flanks and the big horse took off.

Grace and I followed in a rapid gallop across the fields. We leapt the hedges and I felt my pulse race in exhilaration. It struck me that I enjoyed Charles' company, despite my misgivings about him. His odd behaviour, the darkness I sensed in him, his quiet ways … none of that mattered in that instant. I might regret it later; but for the moment, I immersed myself in the motion of the mare, the sting of the cold air and the feel of my muscles warmed with exercise.

Charles brought Raven to a halt at the top of a knoll. I stopped beside him. There was a fine view of Bowerly Hall, the fields and gardens and the sea beyond.

'It is very beautiful,' I said.

'It is my home,' he said simply.

My home too. For better or worse. I gripped Grace's reins tightly. I would not give way to emotion. Weren't things getting better? I had a friend in Peggy. I loved Mary. Now Mrs Dane had mellowed a little. Gradually, it was improving. My homesickness was still there but muted.

'How is my daughter?' Charles asked.

You could always see for yourself... I couldn't say it. He was the Viscount. He owned Bowerly Hall and its vast estate lands. Of course he was busy. Men like him had little time to devote to their children. But what Mary needed was her father's attention. So far, I had seen little evidence that he provided it. She was called down for a few minutes before her bedtime to say goodnight. That was all.

'She is well,' I told him. 'She enjoys nature walks and French, she has a talent for watercolours, and she hates playing the pianoforte.'

He surprised me by laughing.

'What is it?'

'Only that I too hate playing the pianoforte. I can't stand hearing it, either. How strange that Mary should also.'

'If you would talk to her …' I suggested.

The shadows descended. I had come to know that look. It brooked no discussion. Charles shut himself off from the world.

'Mary doesn't need me. She has her grandmamma to talk to, and her governess to teach her what is right and wrong. Your job is to make sure my daughter turns into a well-bred young lady fit for her husband when she is grown. Mary must learn to play music and sing whether she likes to or not.'

'That is rather harsh,' I said. 'Cannot there be more to her life at her tender age than preparing her for a husband?'

'Are you to tell me that your childhood was any different?' he challenged. 'Is that not the way for all young ladies of gentle birth?'

My childhood had been unusual. My father had not prepared me well for the marriage mart. The irony was that he had instead given me knowledge, meaning I was an excellent governess.

'Along with accomplishments, there must be love.'

'Love?'

I blushed and looked down at my hands. What did I mean? I struggled to explain.

'I believe that Mary's health is best served by learning, and being surrounded by people who love her.'

'Do you think my daughter lacks love?' he said shortly.

'No ... not that she lacks it, but ... she needs to be shown it.'

'What do you suggest, Miss Thorne?' Was that a hint of humour in his voice?

I risked a glance at him. The side of his mouth was quirked. Yes, he was laughing at me, a little.

'I think it would be good for Mary if

you spent some time with her. Played a game, or read her a story,' I said boldly. Nothing ventured, nothing gained.

There was a silence. Charles stared out across his lands. A scattered band of crows streaked across the tops of an ancient oak. Their raucous cawing reached us on the breeze. My hair tickled my cheek. I realised it had loosened from its style during the ride. I tucked it in as best I could. Only to find his attention on me.

'Mary doesn't need me,' he repeated firmly.

Then, when I refused to agree, he picked up Raven's reins and pressed his boots to the horse's flanks. 'Let us go back now. I have work to do.'

There was nothing for it but to follow him back across the grass to the stables. I wasn't going to give up, though. He was wrong. His daughter did need him.

There was a carriage at the front entrance to Bowerly Hall. A rather grand one, gleaming and brightly coloured with heraldry. As we drew near, a couple descended from it. Charles led his horse and went over to greet his visitors. I followed, unsure of what to do. Grace's warm breath tickled my neck as I led her. I was conscious of my hair, curls escaping from under my hat. My riding habit was flecked with mud and stems of grass from our ride.

The young woman looked at us. She was beautifully dressed in the latest fashions. Her dress was blue with ribbons and furbelows. Her bonnet was excellently trimmed with matching ribbons. She carried a delicate parasol to complement her outfit. The worst thing was, I recognised her. We had been friends of sorts. She had visited with me at Chelmley, and I in turn had been invited to her home.

'Charles, how good it is to see you,' the man said heartily.

Charles shook his hand and welcomed them both. Politely, he drew me forward and introduced me too. The young man bowed, and the woman inclined her head briefly, as if we had never met before. Then she linked her arms with her beau and Charles, and swept them towards the door with a tinkling laugh.

If I had queried my place in the world, I knew it certainly now. If my father hadn't died, if my aunt and uncle had been different people, I would have been in her shoes. I too would have stepped gaily in my gorgeous clothes and married well, confident of my wealth and status.

I returned Grace to the groom who had appeared to lead Raven back to the stables. Feeling unsettled and strangely bereft, I went to find Mary.

7

Sarah and Charlotte came to call, but I took them away from the Hall. I did not want them to catch the illness that plagued Bowerly. Mary and I walked with them through the walled garden and along the cliff path. The two girls held hands and skipped along. Sarah and I walked more sedately, our heads together, talking.

'Look what James has given me,' Sarah said, showing me a small leather-bound book with gilt letters on its front cover. 'It's his favourite poetry. He says he hopes it will be mine too.' Her face shone.

I hoped for Sarah's sake that James would ask for her hand soon. They were made for each other.

'It is lovely,' I said, sharing her pleasure.

'Are you and Mary quite well?' Sarah asked. 'How awful that Bowerly is in the grip of illness.'

'That's a good way to describe it. Once the fever has burned out, the patients require days of rest to recover. Mrs Dane is exhausted, and so is Peggy. Luckily, the butler hasn't caught it, although both footmen are sick.'

'How are the family coping?'

'Admirably. Lady Anne is tougher than she looks. She has ordered Mrs Bell to simply lay out the food in the kitchen, and she and Charles go down to help themselves. It's like one long picnic in the house.'

'Charles?' Sarah said archly, raising an eyebrow at me.

I felt the heat rise in my face. 'Oh, I meant His Lordship, of course. It was a slip of the tongue, nothing more.'

She placed her hand on my arm. 'Amelia, dear, it's me you're talking to. I hope I am your friend. I certainly consider you to be mine. We must have no secrets between us. Do you really think of him as 'Charles'?'

'He is not the ogre I initially believed him to be,' I admitted. 'He can be abrupt and a little sombre, but there is more to him than that. I truly believe it to be so.'

Sarah smiled, but said no more on the matter. I was keen to change the subject, too. I described the dinner I'd attended, and the appearance of Francis Williams.

'You must keep your distance from him,' Sarah warned.

'Why?'

She looked uncomfortable. 'I've heard rumours. The village girls don't want to work there. He has trouble keeping staff.'

'That must make life hard for his mother. I got the impression that she's an invalid.'

'I believe the poor lady has nervous troubles,' Sarah said.

'How awful for her.'

'Mrs Williams had a hysterical fit in church once,' Sarah said. 'It was horrible. It was as if she was reacting to the sermon my father gave that day. Well, if messages about honour and truth and the consequences of having neither make her flinch, then I say she has something to hide!'

'That does sound very strange,' I agreed.

'People say that the apple hasn't fallen far from the tree when it comes to her son. Be careful.'

'You need have no fear,' I promised her. 'I have no intention of seeking him out.'

'Good.' She looked relieved.

We had reached the part of the cliff walk where the stone steps cut away. Sarah sighed and hugged her book of poetry close to her chest.

'Charlotte and I must leave you now.'

'Won't you join us on the beach?'

'I can't. I must arrange the flowers for church. I hope you don't catch the fever. Come and see us when you can.'

Mary and I waved until they were out of sight. Then, carefully holding hands, we went down the steps onto the beach. It was quite a different atmosphere to the night I'd been pushed to the sand by an unseen person. The last few steps were still slimy, though. I had remembered that correctly. I guided Mary around the seaweed until she hopped onto the sand with a giggle.

I was aware of a thrill at being on this forbidden beach. Neither Charles nor Lady Anne wanted me to be here. I didn't know why. It looked perfectly serene. The sands were neither golden nor red, but somewhere in between. It was quite stony in places, and I spied a few rock pools that I thought Mary might like. The beach overall was a long, thin strand, and at both ends there was a spit of land with a rocky bluff. I looked to the sea. It was well out. There was no chance of being stuck. I could see at once that the stone steps were the only way up. Both bluffs were too craggy to climb, especially in a dress.

'Come on, Amelia!' Mary cried, running along the sand, arms flung high and her bonnet half off her head. 'Come and find some shells.'

'There are shells right here,' I called after her, but she wasn't listening.

I ran, too, to keep up with her. She was midway along the beach before she stopped. I was panting. She held up a white scallop in triumph.

'Look at the size of this one! And there's more of them.' She knelt on the beach and began to gather up the shells.

I stopped and stared. Not at the scallops, but at what lay behind Mary's small figure. I now knew why the lantern had appeared to move up the cliff before vanishing. There were caves here. Two dark entrances loomed in the white chalk of the cliff face. Whoever had come here had simply stepped up and into them. Thus the lantern had gone up too. Like a magic trick, an illusion.

Mary was happy with her finds. She began to build a sandcastle and decorate it with pieces of shell and little pebbles. I went across to the dark holes that gaped in the stone. The cave entrances were slimy green where the sea had entered. It was hard to see much beyond a few feet. I shivered. How horrible to be caught in there by the tide! How high did the sea rise into them? How far back did they go? Was I brave enough to venture inside to find out?

'Mary!' a man's voice shouted.

I stumbled back from the caves, catching my heel on a rock. Charles was making his way along the beach towards us. I tensed, ready for his anger. He'd told me plainly that the beach was out of bounds. What would he do now, finding us here?

I was ready with my excuses — although not with an apology — when Charles put up his hand to stop me. Mary was crouched over her sandcastle. She was silent, watching her father. We both waited. The rushing sound of water as the sea swelled and crashed onto the beach was our backdrop. There was a scent of ozone and a fresh tang to the air. It ruffled Charles' dark hair.

'What have you there, Mary?' He crouched down to her level, oblivious to the fact that his fine breeches would be dampened by sand.

She lifted a pearly shell hesitantly.

'It's a fine castle that you've made. I used to enjoy making these when I was your age.' His voice was warm and casual.

I watched as Mary's back relaxed, and slowly she handed him the shell. Just as solemnly, Charles took it and placed it on top of the sandcastle. He took up an empty horse mussel that Mary had gathered. Using it as a small trowel, he began to scoop sand and build another castle. Seeing him, Mary too picked a shell and dug with it. For a while, there was nothing but companionable silence.

I wasn't needed. Not right then and there. I wandered away from father and daughter, down to the edge of the sea. The water was liquid turquoise. It slurped and puddled on the darkened grains beneath. A few strands of seaweed lifted and lowered with the incoming tide, like black strands of hair. It was very peaceful.

Why was Charles here? Dared I hope he'd taken my advice regarding Mary? As if he'd heard my thoughts, he called over to me.

'Miss Thorne, will you join us? Have you ever had the delight of creating your own stately house?'

'I'm not sure that I have,' I said. 'But I should very much like to live in a castle with high towers and seashell gates.'

'Ah, then you must become an expert builder of such a place. Perhaps Mary will share her secrets with you. She has made a fine palace with a seaweed moat.'

Mary swelled with pride. I noticed she flicked little glances at her father as they played together. She then copied his movements. If Charles laid a whelk in a certain place on his creation, then Mary must likewise have a whelk just so. I hid a smile. This was good for her. Very good. Her little face glowed with all the attention. She was a very different girl from the wan figure who had greeted my arrival. I was pleased. Peggy and I had worked hard to feed her well. I had tried, too, to present her with interesting lessons to stimulate her enthusiasm. But nothing could help the child flourish as much as attention from her parent.

I was pleased with Charles, too. Despite his protests that Mary didn't need him, beach to the steps. It was a long way up to the path above. Somehow Charles was going to have to climb the steps himself. I would go behind in case he fell.

'Mary, I need you to go first. Your father can follow you. Make sure you walk carefully and keep well away from the edge. Can you do that for me?'

She nodded again. For a moment, her serious little face reminded me of Charles. Yes, she had her mother's colouring and prettiness, but there was steel there too. She was going to be a remarkable woman one day, I thought.

We reached the bottom step. Mary trod lightly over the seaweed to the relative safety of the second step.

'Good,' I said. 'Now, keep well in so that you're touching the earth on the left. Never leave it. Should you slip ...' My voice faded. It didn't bear imagining. Then I gave myself a mental shake. If Mary could be brave and hide her fears, then I could too. We were going to get Charles home, even if it took a long, slow walk to do it.

something I had said had penetrated. Otherwise, why was he here? Above our circle of bodies and sand, the entrances to the caves gaped. Charles had not mentioned them. Neither had I. Mary had no interest in them. It was as if they simply weren't there.

A suspicion rose in my mind. What if he was here to distract me from exploring the caves? I could hardly leave the game of sandcastles and walk into the entrances. I was certain he'd stop me. For some reason, I didn't want to ask about them out loud. Then I was annoyed. Was that all this was? Was Charles here not for Mary's sake, but to block me? If that was the case, then I was sadly disappointed in him.

Hot on the heels of these emotions came another thought, hot and sharp as a flying arrow. What was in those caves? What was Charles trying to hide?

'Amelia, look, my palace is finished. Isn't it lovely?' Mary cried.

I forced my mind to focus on the sand creations, to leave the buzz of speculation behind. It was difficult. I longed to stride into the cave and climb up to whatever lay beyond.

'It's marvellous, well done. Can you show me how to make a bridge like yours over the moat?'

Confidently, Mary leaned over to shape me a bridge. Charles caught my eye above her head and smiled. My traitorous heart beat faster. Whatever suspicions I had about him, he had an effect on me. I should be glad that he was spending time with Mary, whatever the motivation for it.

A grey gull cut the air with its piercing call. It circled above us before flying gracefully out to sea. A sudden wind rose up. It brought goosebumps to my skin. Mary shivered.

'I think it's time we went back,' I said to her.

'No, no!' She shook her head with determination, 'I want to stay here — please Amelia, please.'

'You're cold,' I said firmly. 'I don't want you to catch a chill or bring the

fever down on you. Come along n

I looked to her father for sup But Charles was staring at the san gaze unfocused. His brow was white beaded with sweat. As I watched, he unsteadily and groaned.

'Are you quite well, Your Lordship said.

'I don't feel very … quite suddenly . must go back to the house … a seat ..

He staggered against me and I he him. His body was hard and heavy, fo he was much taller than I. A searing hea came from him, and I realised he had the fever. I managed to keep him upright.

'Lean on me; Mary and I will help you back to the house.'

He didn't answer, but gave another groan. Mary looked terrified. The sand-castles were abandoned and she stood beside me. She took her father's hand.

'That's it,' I said to her. 'We must look after your father. He's not well and we must help him to get home.'

She nodded seriously. I was proud of her. Together, we stumbled along the

Mary stepped up once more. Now it was Charles' turn. He was mumbling to himself. It was unclear whether he heard me.

'Now, Your Lordship, you must take care and climb up slowly. Follow Mary, and I will come behind you. If you must halt at any stage, that is fine. We have all day.' I prayed we would not need it.

He lurched up the steps. I breathed in deeply. He had not fallen. There was hope for the rest of the way. I tugged at his sleeve, trying to make him lean into the cliff as I had ordered Mary to do. If he swung in the other direction, I had no way of stopping him falling off. Thankfully, he seemed to understand this. I saw him use all his strength to climb upwards. The sweat poured off him. His dark hair was wet with it. His face was chalky white. With grim determination, he kept going.

How we made it back to Bowerly, I cannot now describe. We met no-one along the way. There were no gardeners in the walled garden to hear a cry for help.

What was a stroll when one was well and healthy had become a struggle.

'Well done,' I said to Mary as we reached the doors. 'I could not have done this without you.' I meant it. Mary looked pleased with my praise, but worried about her father. She had not stopped holding his hand since we reached the cliff top. It comforted him. Now, though, I told her to go inside and find Peggy.

I guided Charles into the cool interior and onto a chair. He dropped his head to his hands as if it was too heavy to hold up. Peggy came running. She stopped when she saw her master in such a state.

'He's got the fever,' I said. 'We must get him upstairs and into his rooms.'

'Oh dear, not His Lordship too. How will we move him?'

'One of us on either side of him. We'll prop him up as he walks.'

Peggy was much the same height as me. Charles leaned his weight on both of us. He was a big man. I felt pain in my shoulders, but bit my lip. It was nothing compared to the fever. I heard Peggy puffing in and out. She was slight, too. It was a strain for both of us.

We managed to get him into his bed-chamber and onto the bed. He closed his eyes and slept. His clothes were soaked. I pulled off his boots. Foolishly, we had dropped him on top of the covers. There was no way I could pull them out from under him.

'Peggy, we need more coverlets, more blankets, can you bring some please?'

'Yes, of course,' she said. 'We'll likely need water and cloths too to cool His Lordship's brow. Someone will have to let Lady Anne know he's ill. Oh, and we should build up the fire.'

'Are the other housemaids back to work?'

'Yes, but on light duties only. I don't want to ask either of them to heft a bucket of coal upstairs. And they're not fit for looking after him. What if they caught the fever again?'

'I don't know if it's possible to catch it twice.' I frowned.

I had no idea if it was possible or not.

One look at Peggy, and I saw that she was frightened. It was little wonder. The whole structure of Bowerly Hall was collapsing because of the fever. Mrs Dane was doing a fantastic job keeping it going. If she fell ill, I hated to think what would happen. The butler was still healthy, but the two footmen were not yet back on duty. Mrs Bell, despite her headache, had not succumbed. The outdoor staff were coming down with it like flies. I supposed that was why there were no gardeners at work.

I forced a cheerful confidence into my voice.

'Looks like it's just us then, Peggy. If you could, please bring up the coal and then a bowl of water and clean cloths. I will arrange for Mary to go and see her grandmamma.'

'But who will nurse His Lordship?' Peggy said, looking confused.

'As there is no-one else to do so, I will.'

8

It was lucky I had not known in advance what I had committed myself to. Charles was not an easy patient. The fever hit him hard. He tossed and turned, murmuring in his slumber. I did my best to restrain him to the bed. He fought me, unknowing. I ducked his flailing fists. Peggy brought bowls of fresh water and I dabbed at his forehead, trying to cool him. I was exhausted when Mrs Dane called to me. I left him and hurried into the hallway.

'How is he?' she asked.

'Not well at all,' I said, 'the fever is very strong. I feel helpless, to be quite honest. What is to be done?'

'You must not panic,' she said in her quiet, cool tones. 'You are doing well. Look after him the way you did for my maids, that is all you can do.'

Her reassurance calmed me. I was

ashamed then that I had showed such emotion. I wanted to be self-controlled like the housekeeper. There was warmth in her eyes as she smiled at me. I think a little of what I was thinking must have shown on my face.

'Don't underestimate yourself, Miss Thorne,' she said gently. 'Now, Lady Anne asks for your presence in the drawing room. Can His Lordship be left alone for a half-hour?'

'I believe so, yes. He is asleep again.'

I went downstairs to find Lady Anne pacing the cluttered drawing room like a caged tiger. She rushed to me.

'Tell me, is there any change in him? Is he better?'

You could come and see for yourself. I swallowed the words back. The sickroom was not for everybody. It took a strong stomach.

'There is no change, I'm afraid. He is in the grip of the fever.'

'Oh, my poor boy.' She pressed her fingers to her lips in distress. 'I must call for the doctor. He must bring a cure immediately.'

There was no cure. If there had been, the doctor would have brought it for Edna and Lil. And what about all the other servants who were ill? Lady Anne hadn't mentioned them. No, there was no other way. Charles must endure the illness like everyone else. But of course I didn't say this to his mother.

'I have sent Mary to the nursery with Peggy,' Lady Anne said. 'I pray and hope she does not catch the illness.'

I hoped so too. Charles was a big, strong man who would probably come through this. But Mary was small and thin. I didn't want to dwell on it. *I must be practical*, I told myself. *I must emulate Mrs Dane.* It was hard to hide my anxiety. Yet hide it I did.

'And dear Francis!' Lady Anne was saying. 'I must send word to my sister-in-law that they simply must not visit us until this dreadful fever has quite vanished. They aren't ill with it, are they?'

She clutched my arm as if I knew.

'I haven't heard otherwise, my Lady,'

I said.

'When did Charles become ill? I don't understand it. He was quite well that morning before he went for his walk. Although I noticed he did not eat much breakfast.'

'It came upon him abruptly when we were at the beach,' I said, without thinking.

She frowned and turned accusing eyes to me. 'What were you doing at the beach? Did I not advise you to stay with Mary in the woodlands and the meadows? I am most disappointed in you, Amelia.'

'His Lordship was playing with Mary,' I said, 'building sandcastles and talking. Maybe it was wrong of me to take her, but she was in no danger there.'

I thought of the dark and sinister caves with their dripping seaweed walls. No, there had been no danger for Mary. But if I had gone into the caves ...

'Charles was playing with Mary?'

She sounded surprised.

I nodded. 'Yes, they had a lovely time until His Lordship became unwell. In

126

fact, Mary was a huge help in getting her father back to the house. She led the way very confidently.'

Lady Anne's eyebrows rose further at this news. Then she sighed.

'I'm prepared to overlook the incident. It sounds as if no harm was done. But promise me you will not venture there in future. It is … unsafe.'

I had no intention of promising any such thing. I was drawn to the cliff, the hewn steps and the secluded beach with its mysterious caves. It was like promising not to breathe. Luckily, at that very moment, Mrs Dane knocked on the door and came in.

'I have sent for the doctor, Your Ladyship. He should be here very soon.'

'Thank you, Mrs Dane. Can you ask Mrs Bell to prepare a light soup for His Lordship, please? He must eat something.'

I doubted Charles was in a fit state to eat. But I understood that Lady Anne needed to feel useful. It was difficult simply waiting for the fever to break.

'Will you go back upstairs, Amelia,

dear? Tend to him. Tell him I send my best wishes for his recovery. But don't ask me to visit until he is better. I really can't. It reminds me too much of Catherine.'

Catherine. Charles' beautiful wife, who had died of a similar fever. I understood Lady Anne's reticence then. There had been illness at Bowerly Hall before, and it had not ended happily. She had lost her daughter-in-law — and her son, too, for a long while.

I was to be reminded of Catherine again when I went back upstairs. Charles was semi-conscious and delirious. The room was stifling. Peggy had made up the fire and it burned brightly. The heavy velvet curtains were drawn and the place was airless. I almost choked on the melding of coal smoke and sickness. As I went to open a window, Charles called out.

'Come to me, come to me, for pity's sake.'

I rushed to his side. His eyes flew open. His hands gripped my upper arms painfully tightly.

'Catherine!' he cried out. 'Catherine,

where are you? Damn it, I need you …'

He dropped back onto the twisted pillows. He moaned and fell asleep. I wished with all my heart that the doctor would arrive. When I heard the front door, I gave silent thanks. The doctor had an air of arrogance, like all such great men. He stroked his bushy grey beard as he frowned at his patient. Then he removed his glasses and rubbed them on his waistcoat. He smelt of liniment and naphthalene.

'Leave us,' he ordered with a clipped impatience.

Reluctantly, I did as I was told. But I stayed outside in the hall, not too far away. Soon enough, the door opened, and I was beckoned back inside.

'He has the same fever as the others,' the doctor said, as if imparting some important news.

I could have told him that myself without any medical training. I nodded as if taking it in.

He coughed importantly. 'You must keep his fever down until it breaks. He will need rest and nourishment thereafter. I have left medicine on the cabinet there. I will call back tomorrow.'

He didn't wait for my answer. He picked up his weighty black bag and his overcoat, and swept out of the sickroom. I paused. Charles was still asleep. At least he was getting some rest. I picked up the blue bottle and shook it. Removing the cork, I took a sniff. It was some mixture of laudanum. I stoppered it and put it back on the cabinet. I was not going to give it to Charles. He was drowsy with fever. He did not need further drowsiness.

I stayed with him for hours, sitting on a chair beside the bed. He slept for much of it. I nodded off at one point, nearly falling off my perch. Then the fever began again, and once more he thrashed around. He called out in his delirium.

'Amelia … Amelia …'

The sound of my name on his tongue was sweet to me. Being logical, I knew he didn't know what he was saying. Normally, he politely called me 'Miss Thorne' in the correct fashion. Just as I would never dream of calling him 'Charles' — except to myself.

'I am here,' I whispered to him, and pressed a cool, wet cloth to his burning forehead.

'Amelia …' He sighed heavily, but seemed then to settle.

It was a very long night. Peggy came in to offer to take my place at his side in the late evening.

'I've finished all my chores,' she said. 'You've had an awful long day of it. Don't you want to leave and get away to bed? I can sit with him.'

'You've had a long day of it, too,' I said, touched by her thoughtfulness. 'I'm alright, really. A little tired, but I have strength yet. How is Mary?'

'She's asleep. It's later than you think. She went to bed a good couple of hours ago. She was very tired, and quite out of sorts.'

'Oh, I had no idea it was so late. I feel guilty at being away from her. But she must understand why.'

Peggy nodded with a cheeky grin, 'Of

course she does. Doesn't mean she has to like it, though. Little madam!'

'She's a good child,' I defended my charge.

'I know she is. Children don't like their routines mucked about with, do they? She'll be right as rain tomorrow, I've no doubt. Oh, I almost forgot — late as it is, Mrs Bell's left a tray of supper for you. Do you want me to bring it up?'

'Mrs Bell made me supper?'

Peggy giggled. 'Don't go getting ideas that she likes you all of a sudden. It was Mrs Dane what ordered her to make it. She was all huffing and puffing, but she didn't dare not make you up some food. Not when Mrs Dane's got her eagle eye on her.'

'I suppose it was too much to hope for, that Mrs Bell has thawed towards me.' I grinned back at Peggy, and we shared our humour.

'You get to your bed, too. I'll be fine. If I need you in the night, I'll come and wake you,' I added.

'Very well. Make sure you do. There's

no good if you fall ill, an' all.' With that warning, Peggy winked and left me to it.

She was right. I had to take care not to catch the fever. It wouldn't help anyone if I did so. I felt that I had my place at Bowerly Hall now. I was important to Mary. I was a friend to Peggy. I hoped I was a useful support to Mrs Dane. Lady Anne was harder to read. Sometimes she was friendly, and I was reminded of her link to my darling mother. At other moments, she could be rather distant, and at those times I was all too clearly conscious of being only the governess. As for Charles, Lord Bowerly, the Viscount … Did I dare to hope that I meant something to him?

The morning brought change. I woke up with a painful crick in my neck from sleeping in the chair all night. Charles was awake. I was aware of my dishevelled appearance, my loose hair and sleep-lined face. He smiled. The fever had broken. He was no longer delirious, nor in a stupor.

'How are you?' I said, stupidly.

'I am much better. I'm sure I have you to thank for that,' he replied softly.

'Not at all,' I said. 'You must thank your own strong constitution for fighting off the infection. There was nothing to be done.'

'I was aware of cool hands tending me.'

'I had to bring the fever down with cold water and sponges.'

'So practical. But you didn't leave me, did you? I felt comforted by your presence.'

Did he remember how he'd called out my name? *And hers. He is still in love with his dead wife*, I thought.

Awkwardly, I got up. My limbs were stiff and my head ached. I longed for a hot bath and a cup of tea. The door was flung open and Peggy stood there, agitated.

'Begging your pardon, Your Lordship, Amelia ...'

'What is it?' I felt the tension rise at her panicked expression.

'It's Miss Mary, I can't rouse her. She's ... I think she's ...' Peggy gulped and tears sprang to her eyes.

I ran from the room and Peggy followed me. I burst into the nursery and straight to Mary's bedroom. She lay there, eyes closed, pale and still. I put my hand to her head, only to find it clammy and cold.

'No wonder she was out of sorts last night,' Peggy sobbed. 'She was sickening for the fever. I'm so stupid, I should've realised something was wrong.'

'It's not your fault,' I reassured her. 'You've been a huge help, looking after her. She's very fond of you. Now, you must dry your eyes, we have work to do. Please fetch water and more blankets.'

Peggy rushed away, almost colliding with a tall figure on her way out. Charles walked unsteadily over to Mary's bed.

'You should not be up, you're not strong enough,' I said. 'Please, Your Lordship, go back to bed. Let me help you.'

But he brushed me gently aside and knelt beside his child. He stroked her hair and Mary murmured in her sleep.

'This is what I have dreaded. I lost Mary's mamma to a fever, and now I may lose my only child too ...' His voice was anguished.

'Is that why you keep your distance from her?' I asked tentatively.

He nodded. 'The pain of losing a loved child ... after losing Catherine, I couldn't bear it. It was easier to disassociate myself from Mary. If I didn't know her too well, then if I lost her, would it not be easier to survive?' He groaned and put his arms around the sleeping girl. 'How could I have thought that? Now, if I lose her, it will be forever in my memory that I did not make full use of the time we had.' His dark head fell forward onto her pillow, his hair mingling with her brighter locks.

I didn't know what to say to ease his pain. Suddenly, I understood him. Under his stiff exterior lay a heart of passion. It was simply that he was afraid to show it. He had lost so much. I felt ashamed of myself for feeling jealous of the Lady Catherine. If my wishes could have come true, I'd have brought her back for him.

To reunite the little family. To bring Mary her dear mother back, and Charles his soulmate. For that was how I saw them now.

I slipped quietly out of the room. I wanted to allow Charles to be alone with Mary; for, soon, I would have to nurse her the way I had her father.

Downstairs, all was in an uproar. Mrs Dane's voice rose as she barked orders at the flustered maids. Peggy had a bowl of sloshing water in her arms. She looked as if she didn't know what to do. The other girls fled before Mrs Dane's clicking footsteps.

'Peggy, what are you doing? I require you to dust and polish upstairs. Right now.'

'Oh, but, Mrs Dane ...'

'Don't answer back, girl. Hop to it. Put that bowl of water down and find the dusters.'

Peggy threw me a frightened look and hurried off. The bowl of water was left on a small table. The butler glided across the polished floor, a sheaf of papers in hand. One of the footmen took a tray of bottles and pushed through the dining room doors.

'What is going on?' I asked Mrs Dane.

'Mrs Williams and her son are arriving this afternoon. Quite unexpected. The house is in no fit state for a visit.'

She had just finished speaking when Lady Anne came swiftly towards us, looking distressed.

'How is Mary? Peggy has told me she is not well. Please tell me she hasn't caught the fever!'

'I ... I don't know yet. His Lordship is with her. I will tend to her with utmost care, and I'll send Peggy with a message once I've checked Mary properly.' For some reason, I was reluctant to say that the fever had struck again. If I said it, it made it so. I held my tongue on such a pronouncement. I wanted to see Mary and hopefully to wake her and get her to take some sustenance.

'Lady Anne, Mrs Williams and your nephew have sent a message to say they will visit with you this afternoon,' Mrs Dane said politely.

Only her stiff posture gave away her annoyance. She was too good a housekeeper to complain about the inconvenience.

'Oh, no.' Lady Anne waved her hands in agitation, 'No, that won't do at all. They mustn't come to Bowerly. What if Francis was to get ill? I would never forgive myself. You must send a message by return and tell them not to come. Tell them of the fever. Besides, Charles is in no fit state to receive guests. He is still weak. Make sure there are no visitors this week, Mrs Dane.'

She went away into a side room, calling for breakfast to be brought. I think, in her distress, she had forgotten that Mrs Bell was still soldiering on without much help. Breakfast would not be a feast.

Mrs Dane gave a small smile. 'That's a relief. I didn't think it was right for the Williamses to visit, but they're not easily put off when they choose to come here. Only the fear of illness will keep them at bay.'

She went looking for a footman to carry a message across the fields. I took the bowl of rapidly cooling water, and went back upstairs to see Mary. Charles had gone — I hoped, back to his own recuperation. Mary was awake. She blinked sleepily and smiled at me.

'Papa was here with me. I felt him cuddle me close. Or was it a dream?'

She was pale, and there were lilac shadows under her eyes, like bruises. Her nose was running. I handed her a clean handkerchief.

'It wasn't a dream,' I said. 'Your papa was here. He loves you very much, and he's concerned.'

'What about?' She sneezed and blew her nose.

I had another handkerchief, which I passed to her. A sneaking suspicion crossed my mind.

'Do you feel hot? Or shivery?'

She shook her head. 'No, but I have a headache, and my nose is stuffed.' She sneezed again.

Mary didn't have the fever. She had a common cold. I was certain she had no hot forehead, and there were no signs of muscle weakness or chills. With a wave of relief, I told her to rest.

'Why can't I get up?' Her lower lip wobbled dangerously.

'You can get up,' I said. 'But I want you to go slowly today. We won't go outside, we'll play indoors quietly. I can read you some books, and we can have a game of cards. Would you like that?'

She nodded and yawned. 'I do want to do that. Can I lie here a little bit first?'

'You do that. I have to go and see your papa.'

I hurried along the corridor to tell Charles the good news. He was not going to lose his daughter. It would do them both good to spend a morning slowly reading and playing together.

9

I spent one of the happiest days of my life with Charles and Mary. He had bathed and dressed when I went back upstairs after a small breakfast. He was as pale as Mary, and both had dark circles under their eyes. But the atmosphere was peaceful and contented. He had his papers and sat reading them. Mary was sitting up in bed, playing with her dolls.

I went over to the windows, intending to open them. Fresh air was beneficial to my patients. But it was a cold, blustery day outside. The sky was dull pewter-grey. Rain splattered the glass ceaselessly. Beyond, I made out the stormy sea with white waves abundant.

It was a good day to stay inside. I drew my shawl over my shoulders, glad of its warmth. A letter had arrived from Mrs Bidens. I read it sitting next to Mary's bed.

My dearest Amelia,

Thank you for your letters. I am sorry I have not written to you in reply. I suppose I wanted to give you time to settle into your new life. I did not want to remind you of what you had left behind.

However, you sound happy at Bowerly Hall, and I hope that is so. How is Anne? I would love to see her again. It has been many years since we last met. Your description of Mary paints a picture for me of a clever young lady. She must be a joy to teach. You don't mention Charles. I presume you must not see much of him. As master of the house, he must be kept very busy.

I wonder if you have met Anne's sister-in-law? I recall the brother was something of a family black sheep, but I won't spread gossip and tell you why. He was much in London before his early demise, and of course everyone knew of him. I never met his poor wife. She stayed in the country and never came up to town. There was a son.

Perhaps you have met him? Though if he is anything like his father, then I should hope that your paths have not crossed.

I am kept very busy at present. My cousin is in poor health. She lives in London — but in a far nicer area than mine! I travel to care for her daily, but it is tiring. London is such a bustling place, so crammed with horses and carriages and people that it is hard to breathe.

I must leave this letter now, as the candle is almost gone. I think about you often and pray that you are well. Remember, my dear, there is always a home for you here if it is needed.

Yours

Hannah Bidens

Dear Mrs Bidens. It was kind of her to offer her home to me. It was reassuring that if my position here at Bowerly were to fail, I had somewhere to go. It could only be for a short while, of course. Mrs Bidens couldn't afford to keep me. And I could not afford to be without some form of paying employment. Still, I comforted myself, London was — as she noted — a very large city. There would be employment to be had.

I looked across the room to where the rain trickled down the windows. The nursery was a high-ceilinged draughty room. Dark wood panelling on each wall didn't help the quality of light. The whole of Bowerly Hall had a somewhat gloomy aspect. And yet I had grown to love it here. I realised that I didn't want to go back to London.

'What shall we play?' Mary asked, putting her dolls down.

'We could use your tea set and make afternoon tea for your dolls. Or I could read you a story. What would you prefer?'

'Can we do both?'

'You can choose what we do today.'

'Will there be no lessons at all?' She squeezed her hands together hopefully.

I laughed. 'No lessons. Instead, you must promise to get well. Peggy will bring you some food soon, and I want you to eat it all up. Will you do that for me?'

She nodded, then slyly looked to her father. He was engrossed in a set of newspapers which had arrived.

'Will Papa have to eat all his food too?'

He moved the papers down so that he could see her. His brow quirked in a mock frown.

'What's this? What am I to be forced to do?'

Mary looked gleeful. 'You have to do what Amelia says, all day. Just like me.'

'Indeed.' Charles' gaze flickered to my face and he looked amused. 'And what will you have me do, Amelia?'

So I was no longer 'Miss Thorne'. He obviously felt he knew me well enough to use my given name. Unless it was because of the informality of the nursery environment.

'I will have you take care of yourself,' I said, pretending to be severe, to hear Mary's delighted giggles. 'I will insist that every scrap of good food that is sent up, is eaten. When you are better, I will insist on long, brisk country walks to build you up.'

To build you up. What nonsense I was gabbling. One look at his powerful shoulders was enough to see he did not need any of that. But he played along as Mary observed us both happily.

'Long country walks? Well, if I must, then of course I shall do so. On one condition.'

'And what condition would that be?' I asked, drawn into the silly game too far.

'That you should accompany me on these long outings.'

Oh, what enjoyment I should have if such a thing were possible! I felt a thrill surge through me — until I dampened it down. We were joking. That was all. It was a game of amusement for Mary. Except that, when I dared raise my head, he was waiting for an answer.

'I … I should like that very much,' I said plainly.

'And I will hold you to it,' he replied.

Mary sighed loudly, trying to pull her father's attention back to her.

'I want my tea set now,' she told me. 'You can be the grandmother, and I will be the lovely lady of the house. My dollies will be our honoured guests. What dainty dishes will we offer them?'

And so the day progressed. A beautiful posy of flowers arrived from Sarah and Charlotte with their very best wishes. I was glad they'd stayed away. The flowers were cheering and took centre stage in the nursery. Their sweet scent wafted in the air.

Charles took his leave of us at midday. He had work to do, and felt fit enough to tackle it. He looked better. His illness had been brief, thankfully. Mary and I spent the afternoon reading and drawing until Peggy brought a tray of dinner for us both.

'She's in a right old mood,' she grumbled, placing the tray on the table next to the bed.

I didn't need to ask who she meant.

'Shouting at me and Edna and Lil. Nothing we do is right. Lil's down there chopping carrots, with Mrs Bell snapping at her to go faster. Edna got into big trouble because the soup burnt over. Then she tells me she's told Mrs Dane I can't have me day off on Sunday! I'm needed, apparently, 'cos she's 'aving a day boiling up puddings. What am I going to tell me Mam? She was relying on me to take me sisters out and give her a rest.'

'She sounds worse than usual.'

'Yes, she is. I don't know why. She ought to be pleased the Williamses aren't arriving after all. She's only feeding Her Ladyship and himself.'

Peggy gave a great sigh and shrugged her shoulders. 'Any road, here's some soup — not too burnt — warmed bread and pork chops. Get that down you, Miss Mary, and it'll make your teeth shine.'

Mary laughed before it ended in a giant cough. She'd gone through a mountain of handkerchiefs. There'd be a lot of laundering needed this evening. She and I tucked into our meal with relish. Soon enough, it was time for her to sleep, and for me to slip away to my rooms.

Once in my sitting room, I couldn't settle. I had not had an active day. I had sat with Mary playing parlour games or flicking through the pages of a storybook. Now I was restless.

One of the maids had made up a fire. I sat beside it and tried to concentrate on my novel. The words danced in front of me. With exasperation, I flung it down. I went and lay on the bed.

I must have dozed, for I woke with a start. Disorientated, I struggled up. It was pitch black outside. How late was it?

I rubbed my face. I would go downstairs and fetch some hot chocolate. The thought cheered me. It was something to do. Suddenly I craved its thick sweetness. I tidied my hair and smoothed my dress. I slipped on my shoes and went out.

There was no-one about as I headed down to the kitchen. It was clearly very late. I began to think I'd have a wasted journey. Surely there would be no hot chocolate at this hour. I went anyway. There was a light in the kitchen. Mrs Bell jumped when I saw her.

'Oh, what do you want? I'm just ... just locking up before I go to bed. Why are you wandering about so late?'

'Doesn't Peggy usually lock up?' I said.

She scratched her head as if pondering my words. I noticed her bitten-down nails. Her mouth was pursed, and she was twitchy, not keeping still as I watched her.

'Peggy?' she echoed. 'Well, I gave her the night off, didn't I? Told her I'd lock up tonight. Which is what I'm doing. As you can see.'

'She didn't mention she had a night off when I saw her earlier. Only that she wasn't getting her day off on Sunday.' I wanted Mrs Bell to know how unfair I thought she was being on Peggy.

'That's why I gave her tonight off.' There was a triumphant expression on her face, as if she'd tricked me. Her feet tapped impatiently on the flagged stones. 'Why are you down here?'

'I was hoping for some hot chocolate.' Glancing at the sideboard, I saw I was out of luck. There was no silver tray and cups waiting. No smell of sugar.

'There isn't any. Tell you what, if you go back upstairs, I'll bring you a pot on my way up.'

'You will?'

'Yes, yes. Only you need to go up. I'll be ten minutes or so, locking up and so forth.' She waved me away with fluttering hands.

I was so bemused, I let myself be herded from the kitchen. Slowly, I went back upstairs. I paused midway but couldn't hear her.

Back in my sitting room, I sank into the armchair and watched the flames. There was something odd about her behaviour. It was hard to put a finger on exactly what. I waited and waited. At some point, I slept.

What woke me? A creak, or chink of metal? The hairs on the back of my neck rose, and I felt a sense of things being not quite right. I stood up as quietly as possible, straining to hear the noise. There it was. It sounded like metal hitting metal; like tumblers set against each other too fast. And where was my hot chocolate? Mrs Bell hadn't been in to leave it. How very odd.

I tiptoed out into the hallway. There,

I stopped. I had a sense of someone else abroad in the night. Was it my imagination? I breathed shallowly, not wanting to be heard. I moved out and down the stairs. There it came again. A clink of glass being moved. What was going on?

I was not prepared for the reality. Somewhere in my mind, I think I had believed it to be Edna or Lil up in the night, hurrying through extra duties. Preposterous, I knew. But I had to find some reasoning answer.

The truth was far worse.

There was a dark figure in the ground-floor hallway. I gasped, and it turned. I caught a glimpse of a pale face before the intruder ran. I ran too. He or she sped down the stairs to the servants' hall. I hesitated at the top. What if I cornered him? What then? Was I to be faced with violence?

I looked back at the wide hallway. I had interrupted a thief at work. There was a scattering of objects on the carpet: a single candlestick vaguely visible in the shadows, a couple of books, and what looked like the shape of a small painting. The thief was here. He had targeted Bowerly Hall.

Outraged, I ran down after him, through the long dining room and into the kitchen beyond. My leg stung where I hit a chair on my flight along. I came to a sudden stop. The kitchen was empty. Where was he hiding?

I was aware of my own breathing. It was coming fast and shallow from my exertions. I tried to calm it. I wanted to hear other sounds. The room was all shadows and angles. The range was unlit, and the fire banked for the night. It was cold. There was the odour of old ashes and vegetable peelings.

A draught blew across my bare arms and brought up goosebumps. Now I knew why I couldn't find him. Fool that I was! While I was listening for his hiding place, he was no doubt miles away. Because the back door to the kitchen was ajar. I ran to it. The bolts were undone. He'd slipped away before I got there.

I had to get Charles. I retraced my

steps, avoiding the items trailed across the ground- floor hallway. I went to my room and pulled on my shawl. Then I went to wake the Viscount.

'What the … Amelia? What's wrong?' He was immediately alert.

I explained as quickly as possible what I had seen and heard. He grabbed his robe and followed me.

'See,' I said, pointing to the candlestick and other things, 'he's stolen from the library. Goodness knows what else he's taken. He must have dropped these when he heard my footsteps.'

Charles bent to pick up the candle-stick. He stared at it long and hard as if it would reveal all. Then he gathered up the books and the painting and took them into the library. He put them in a heap on the walnut desk.

'We must send for the constable,' I urged him. 'He's getting away. This is our chance to capture the thief that's been plaguing the countryside. What are you waiting for?'

'Show me where he got out.'

Impatiently, I took him down to the servants' hall until we reached the back door. Charles stood and stared until I wanted to shake him. Where was his sense of urgency?

'He must have had inside help,' I said. 'Someone has unlocked the bolts from in here and let him in.'

I couldn't help thinking of Mrs Bell and how nervous she'd been earlier. I didn't like the woman, but that didn't make her a thief. I had to be careful before I accused her of betraying Bowerly. I had no proof it was her. Anyone could have slipped down in the night and undone the bolts and locks. Maybe I was letting my personal feelings get in the way of logical thought.

I was aware that Charles had still not leapt into action. Instead, he was thoughtful.

'Shall I send a boy for the police?' I said.

'No.'

'Why ever not?' I asked in shock.

Then it hit me. I moved back from him

so that I could stare straight up into his eyes. I wanted to see his reaction. Then I spoke.

'You know who the thief is, don't you?'

10

I had to wait for a few days before I left the house. I was due a day off on the Thursday. Time stretched like soft dough. I was kept busy with Mary's lessons, and the weather was foul. It rained and stormed without end. No-one was keen to venture out.

Miraculously, Thursday dawned dry and bright. I picked my stoutest pair of shoes to wear, and took a bag with two candles and a few matches tucked into it. I had promised Sarah that I would visit her — but I was determined to get inside the caves too. Nothing would stop me, I vowed.

I thought of the strange events on the night of the theft. Charles had denied knowing who the intruder was. He had only said that he had his suspicions and would be drawn no further on the matter. His face had been grim but there was worry too, shadowing it. I had urged him to call the authorities, but he was equally adamant he would not.

The next day, Mrs Bell was called to the library by the Viscount. There was a hushed atmosphere amongst the servants. Everyone hurried about their business, eyes lowered, with no chatter or laughter. Peggy described to me later what had happened.

'She came back down to the kitchen ever so quiet. She was that white, we made her sit down and take a glass of water. I've never seen her act so nice since. I don't know what His Lordship said to her, but she's a changed woman.'

'So she is still in her position as cook?' I asked.

Peggy nodded, 'Oh, yes; she got the menu for the week from Lady Anne that day all as normal. Although I do feel the food is fancier, and she's making a real effort, like she's proving herself all over.'

I wondered what Charles had said to her. Had she been threatened with losing her job? Had she given up the name of the thief? Or was she in fact completely innocent? It was exasperating, not knowing what was going on.

'Lil and Edna are in seventh heaven,' Peggy went on with a giggle. 'They've not been shouted at once all week. Even when Edna put salt in the pastry dough instead of sugar. She thought she was in for a belting, but Mrs Bell just told her to make it again proper, like. You should've seen Edna's jaw drop. Honest, it was so funny. I think we could get away with murder down there right now, and she'd not say a word.'

She must have had quite a fright to become so pliant and pleasant.

'Leopards don't change their spots, though, do they? I reckon, give it another week, and she'll be back to shouting and hitting the girls with her wooden spoon when they don't please her.' Peggy sighed.

'You're probably right. Make the most of it while you can.' I smiled.

Now I walked across the meadows and down the lane to the vicarage. The leaves lay scattered under my feet like a russet carpet. The branches of the trees were starkly bare. A mist hung low over the ground, and I smelt the first mushrooms that sprouted round the tree trunks.

Sarah welcomed me with a warm hug and drew me inside.

'I'm so glad to see you,' she said. 'Come in, let me take your bonnet and coat. Will you take tea or chocolate?'

'Tea, please.'

'I'll send for it, and perhaps some freshly-baked biscuits too. How is everyone at Bowerly? I've been so worried about you all.'

'I'm very glad to say that everybody is improving nicely. His Lordship is better, and Mary was lucky and escaped the fever. She has a head cold, but it's not too bad. The servants are all on the mend, too, or so Peggy tells me. She seems to know all that is happening in the house.'

'A lot is happening, so I hear.' Sarah frowned.

'You heard about the thief, then.'

'Yes, indeed. Viscount Bowerly came here to confer with my father. I don't know what was said but father did tell me of the break-in. I do wish whoever it is was caught. I can hardly sleep easily at night because of it.'

'Your father thinks it unlikely that the vicarage will be targeted,' I reminded her gently.

'I know, it's silly of me. I let my imagination run away.'

The tea and biscuits arrived, and we talked of lighter matters while eating and drinking. I had the sense that Sarah had something more to tell me. She was fidgety, nibbling at a biscuit and sipping tea. Sometimes she stopped mid-sentence, as if she'd drifted in her thoughts. At last, I could take it no more.

'Sarah, what is it? There is something on your mind. Will you not share it with me?'

'Is it that obvious?'

I laughed. 'Yes, it is. You've eaten half a biscuit, and broken the rest into crumbs with your fingers. And you've drunk three cups of tea to my one. Tell me what is going on, please.'

Her eyes shone with sudden excitement.

'James has asked to speak to Father tonight after dinner. I ... I think he will ask for my hand in marriage.'

'That is wonderful news,' I said, delighted for my friend. 'He is a lucky man to capture your heart.'

'He most certainly has captured my heart,' she sighed happily. 'But he is the kindest, gentlest man I have ever met, and so I am actually the lucky one.'

There was true love speaking. Sarah looked so pretty, flushed with emotion as she talked about James. How lovely to be in love, and have that love returned. How reassuring it must be to find your soulmate in this world. I was not jealous of Sarah — how could I be, when I wanted the best for my friend?

But a little part of me asked whether I would ever be so blessed. It was unlikely. Governesses were of course spinsters. It was not the work for married women. My future was likely to be that of teaching, and maybe companionship for ladies. The shadow of the poorhouse was ever-present on the horizon, though I prayed it would never come to that. However, I was dependent on the goodwill of my employers over the years to come, and could never lose that sense of slight anxiety.

But it was with a glad heart that I congratulated Sarah, and we spent the next hour happily discussing wedding plans, dresses, food, and other details of the celebrations to come.

'I hope I haven't been too forward in all this,' Sarah said at one point. 'What if James is going to speak to Father on a completely different topic?'

'You cannot have misjudged him so,' I reassured her. 'Of course it will all come right. You must trust in yourself, and in your beloved James. Tomorrow, you must let me know how it all went.'

We had a most pleasant time together until mid-afternoon when I took my leave. I didn't want to be too late getting to the caves. The dusk came ever earlier as autumn progressed. The last thing I wanted was to be caught on that beach in the darkness with the tide coming in … I shivered.

I checked that the candles and matches were still in my bag, then waved goodbye to Sarah. I retraced my steps from the vicarage until I was standing high up on the edge of the meadow at the white stone steps. My heart beat faster in anticipation of adventure. I was convinced there were answers to be found in the caves.

There wasn't a soul about, either in the meadows or on the beach below. The sky had turned to a dull grey, and the wind had whipped up seafoam that scattered across the sand as I walked on it. A few gulls cried mournfully as they sailed high above. I stood on a seashell and heard it crunch. The stink of seaweed stung in my nostrils. Then I was there: standing directly outside the cave entrances.

I glanced out towards the sea. The tide was far out, and the beach stretched in width and length in all its sandy glory. I calculated I had some hours before the tide rushed back in. Now I stared up at the two black holes before me. The green slime coating the stone disgusted me. Somehow, I had to climb into one of them. It took me a moment to gather my courage.

I reminded myself how far I had come in life. I had started as a shy, quiet girl, content to live in Chelmley Wood with Father. Circumstances beyond my control meant I had been torn from that life. I had survived London. I had survived Uncle Timothy's and Aunt Lucy's lack of love and cold home.

I had made a life for myself at Bowerly Hall. There were Mary, Peggy and Sarah for company. Dared I include Charles in my circle of friends? Perhaps. In some ways he was still an unknown quantity. Just as I thought I knew him he'd draw away, closed off and aloof. I had to remember he was a Viscount, and therefore out of reach to me. Yet, in his softer moments, I felt closer to him than to anyone else.

Enough, I chided. None of that was helping me to get inside the caves. I checked that my shoes were tightly laced. It would do no good tripping on them and falling. I looked to the two entrances, unsure which to take. It really didn't matter. It was all chance. So I decided on the left-hand one. Here, the stone was worn to smoothness on the sides, and there was less slime.

Taking a deep, steadying breath, I climbed up onto a pile of blocky stones and pulled up into the lip of the cave. With a shaking hand, I retrieved a candle and struck a match to light it. At once the darkness lifted. The warm orange glow was strangely comforting. It dispersed some of my fear and lit my way. The floor of the cave, now that I was up and into it, was relatively flat. In I walked: into what, I had no idea.

Gradually, the passageway sloped up. The air was much colder. The stone wall was dry to my touch. The candle flickered. I held my breath. *Please, please let the light hold!* I couldn't imagine trying to find my way back out in pitch black. The flame wavered but stayed lit.

The ground beneath my feet began to widen. Soon I was standing in a wide chamber, most of which was in deep shadow. A single candle could not begin to fill the space with light. I pushed it out before me, trying to see where I was.

The candlelight glinted on some objects. I moved forwards. Kneeling, I held the candle over them. All my suspicions had been correct. Here was a treasure trove collected by the thief who had raided the county. There were gold candlesticks, gold plate, crystal bowls and paintings. The more I roved the chamber, the more I saw.

Whoever he was, he was clever. It was an ingenious hiding place for stolen goods. Hardly anyone came to the beach. There was a much better beach, so much easier to access, further down the coast. I was sure very few people knew of the caves. Yet amongst those who knew were Lady Anne and Charles. I had been repeatedly put off from exploring the beach. What was it they were hiding?

I knew what I had to do. I didn't know how involved the Viscount and Dowager Viscountess were in whatever was going on. I didn't know what Mrs Bell's part in all of this was. The only path I could take was to call for the constable. Then the whole mess could be sorted out by the law.

Feeling better with my decision made, I hurried as fast as possible back to the entrance. I didn't need to explore the other passage. Either it held more treasure, or it was empty apart from nature. Either way, the police would take charge. I had had enough of dark draughty caves and the smell of seaweed and salt water.

I had almost reached the exit when my heart stopped in dread. A tall figure blocked the light. There was no way out except past it. And I was visible, holding my candle with its bright flame. There was only one hope: if I ran back into the chamber, perhaps there was another way out ...

'Amelia?'

'Charles? Is that you? You frightened me so.' With relief I went towards him, not stopping to ask why he was there.

Only as I reached him did the thoughts

slide into my head: *Is he the thief? Have I handed my fate to a monster?* But I didn't truly believe that of him. My instinct was to trust him.

Despite that, I couldn't help the question on my lips. 'What are you doing here?'

'I could ask the same of you,' he replied. 'But I think we both know the answer. You couldn't leave it alone. You're too curious for your own good.'

At that, I shrank back. What did he mean?

'What is in there?' he asked. 'Did you find something?'

'I'll show you.'

It was simpler to show him than to try to explain the sheer volume of stuff hidden in the cave. I was very conscious of him behind me as I moved swiftly back the way I had come. If he meant me harm, I had little way of defending myself. He was so much taller, so much stronger physically, than me.

'You should be more careful in your activities,' Charles said sternly.

'If I had not explored the caves, we'd be none the wiser about what is going on,' I argued.

'I would have explored them — that is what I intended today.'

'Why did you think of them?'

'As I explained to you, I have my suspicions as to who the thief is. I have been pondering the mystery of where the stolen items could be. It struck me this is the only secret place around. Unless, of course, the thief sells what he steals immediately. But that is unlikely: it would be difficult to move the goods without notice. No, so much better to let there be a cooling-off time. Once people have forgotten the crimes, then he can prosper from them.'

'How did you know that I'd be here?' I asked.

'I didn't. But I heard Peggy telling Mary you had gone out today, and I suspected you were up to something.'

'I was not 'up to something',' I said indignantly. 'I was actually visiting Sarah Wyckham.'

'Ah, Miss Wyckham at the vicarage. I did not realise you had her acquaintance.'

'Indeed I do, just as you have with her father.'

He chuckled. 'Touché, Miss Thorne. Touché.'

I smiled too in the dark. His good humour lit mine. Then we were there in the chamber and I showed him what I had found.

'I am most sorry to find that my suspicions are true,' he said, bending down to touch the heavy gilt frames of the paintings. 'Hand me the candle, please.'

He looked more closely at the picture. It was a bland landscape, with fields and hedges and a few bored-looking horses.

'I have seen this painting adorn the dining room at Whitehaven Castle. It is priceless. I will be very glad to be able to return it to the family.'

'Priceless? Really?' It was hard to hide my surprise. It was such an ugly painting.

Charles turned and smiled. 'It is not to your taste?'

'Well, I can't say that it is. But I'm not

an art expert, of course.'

'You don't fancy this on your wall?'

'Not at all,' I said firmly, 'I don't care one whit if it is priceless.'

He gave me a strange look then. 'You are a very interesting person, Amelia.'

There was nothing I had to say to that. I wasn't sure what he meant. Then he smiled again and stood straight.

'We should go,' he said. 'It's getting late outside, and we must not get caught by the tide or the dusk.'

'Wait—' I caught his arm, feeling the fine fabric of his jacket under my touch. Reluctantly, I let go. 'You know who the culprit is. You must tell me.'

He hesitated. I stood my ground. I wasn't leaving until I knew the answer. He must have sensed my determination, for he gave a sigh and began to speak.

'I am not one hundred percent certain. Until I am, I will not go to the law. That would be shameful to the one I suspect.'

'And that person is …?'

'My cousin Francis.'

Hearing it said out loud was rather

shocking. It made sense, and fit with my own suspicions — but still, where was the logic? Francis Williams was gentry. He lived in a fine house with his mother. What on earth stimulated him to steal?

Charles explained: 'I know that Francis has a love of gambling. His father was the same before him. I also know that Francis has run up huge debts in London. Several of the gentlemen he owes money to have approached me for help. With some threats, too, if Francis fails to pay up. I have paid what I can. But I cannot pay more. I have Bowerly Hall to consider. I have my own mother to shelter from the truth. Bowerly must not pay for Francis's sins.'

'So you think he has stolen all this to pay off his debts. How does he manage to gain entrance to the estates and houses?'

'I believe he has inside help. In the case of Bowerly, I know it. You were right when you said someone had unbolted the kitchen door to allow the thief entry. It was Mrs Bell. She confessed all when I challenged her.'

'But she hasn't lost her job?'

'There are mitigating circumstances. Francis had a hold on her. Her cousin's husband is a no-good scoundrel by all accounts. Francis threatened to have him put in prison if Mrs Bell didn't help him. As an incentive, he also offered her money — which she needs to support her cousin, apparently. Besides, she is an excellent cook and has been with our family for many years. She is extremely contrite. Lastly, how can I let her go without explaining to my mother why I have done so?'

The cousin would be Mrs Smith, Mary's nanny, who had lost her job when I arrived as governess. What a twisted web of lies and deceit and treachery!

'I don't understand why you haven't told the constable all this.'

'I only have Mrs Bell's word that Francis is to blame. I owe it to my cousin, and to my aunt and my own mother, to prove it before I accuse him of these awful deeds.'

We had reached the fresh air and the

shore. Charles went in front of me and leapt to the sand. He offered his hand and I stepped more gingerly down. Long skirts are quite a hindrance to exploration and climbing.

'How are you going to prove that it's Francis?' I asked.

'By setting a trap,' Charles said.

11

Charles' plan was simple. He put it into action the very next day. A letter of invitation to dinner was sent to the Williams, explaining that Bowerly Hall was now free from fever, and how delighted Lady Anne and Charles would be to entertain their relatives that evening. The footman returned with an acceptance. Francis was delighted to accept their kind invitation, and looked forward to dinner and conversation at eight p.m. Unfortunately, his dear mama was out of sorts, and would not be joining them. She did, however, send her kindest regards, and hoped that Lady Anne would visit her soon.

Mrs Dane found plenty of extra work for the staff in preparation for the event. The housemaids were set to dusting all over. A footman was sent to the village to procure the largest ham possible for Mrs Bell. Peggy complained she'd never seen such a mountain of vegetables to be peeled and washed and cut for the evening meal.

'You'd think it was royalty coming,' she said. 'His Lordship sent a special message for Mrs Bell to make sure it was a fine meal tonight. Nothing but the best to be served up. Mind you, she didn't half sniff at that. Said she always cooks the finest meals, and it won't be no different tonight.'

'I'm sorry it's so much work for the kitchen staff.'

'Oh, don't you worry about that, I'm just having a moan on behalf of Edna and Lil. It's them what'll have to bear the brunt of the work. Once that veg is done, we'll all be happier. Although the dessert is some kind of fruit and meringue construct, it looks like it might explode if touched. I really hope nothing happens to it before it's served up, and I don't envy the footman that has to carry it up the stairs to the dining table.'

Charles clearly wanted his cousin to be contented that night. Then he'd spring his trap.

Lady Anne was beautifully dressed, as always, when I met her at the entrance to the dining room. She was wearing a cream gown embroidered with tiny dusky pink roses. Her hair was swept up and adorned with similar flowers, subtly woven into her braid. Her hands fluttered nervously to her throat where a string of lustrous pearls lay. She did not know that Bowerly Hall had been burgled. Charles felt it would be too much for his mother's health to know. Seeing her, I felt he was right. There was a frailty to her I had not noticed before.

I wished I was not wearing the same green silk I had worn to dinner before; but it was my best dress, and I had no choice. My grey silk was too old, too unfashionable for such an occasion. I would have to hope no-one commented.

'How is Mary? I did not have time to see her today,' Lady Anne said. 'You must bring her to me tomorrow morning instead. We will have cake together.'

'I'm sure that Miss Mary will enjoy that very much. Shall I fetch her for you at eleven?'

'That will do very nicely. Now, come along, we must go in. I hear Francis being welcomed at the front door. It won't do if we are not ready to receive him.'

The dining room was once more set in such a way as to be a pleasure to look upon. The fire burnt brightly and gave off a satisfying warmth. The candles in the chandelier and wall sconces were lit. The same vast range of crystalware and silver cutlery was in place on the snowy white linen of the table. For this meal, the centrepiece was cream and yellow roses with some dark green leaves that I did not recognise, which must have come from a hothouse where nature and the seasons had not cast them aside.

Charles and Francis joined us soon afterwards. I sensed Charles' slight tension in the way he held himself erect. He stood ramrod-straight, as if aware of every movement. Francis, by contrast, sloped into the room and took his seat with barely a greeting. It was a far cry from the charming man who had graced the room last time.

Lady Anne gave a sudden faint cry. 'My dear, your poor face! What has happened?'

He raised a limp hand to stop her. 'It is nothing; you must not fret so, Aunt.'

'It is not 'nothing',' she protested. 'You have a terrible black eye and your cheek is bruised also. What have you done?'

He gazed at us all before answering, with a curl of his lip, 'I had a rather unfortunate fall from my horse. There is nothing to worry about, I do assure you. Now, can we talk of other matters?'

Lady Anne looked as if she'd like to say more. There was something in her expression which made me wonder how much she guessed about her nephew. I had an inkling she knew more than she let on. She had tried to keep me from going to the beach. She had also, I remembered, been unhappy that Francis had visited Mrs Bell during his last dinner here. Would she be quite so protective of her nephew if she knew that he had tried to steal from Bowerly itself?

'My mother is right,' Charles said, 'that is rather a nasty wound to your face, old fellow. Have you had the doctor look at it?'

'What do you care?' Francis snarled. Then he blew out a breath and seemed to make an effort to smile pleasantly. 'Sorry, cousin, the pain of it is causing me to be somewhat on edge. I do apologise. No, I saw no need to rouse the doctor for such a trivial accident. It looks worse than it is.'

'Mrs Dane has an ointment which is most efficacious for such things,' I said. 'If you wish, I could ask her later to bring you some?'

'Goodness, no. Really, it is nothing. Now, please can we talk of better news?'

The first course was served, and none of us spoke until the butler and his footmen had withdrawn. Mrs Bell had excelled herself. There was a thin fish soup with wafer-like toast slices, and it was all most delicious.

I saw Charles slide a glance or two at Francis, a calculating expression on his face. He, like I, was guessing where the bruising had come from. Charles had mentioned Francis's debts. It was likely that the men he owed money to were becoming increasingly angry at his failure to pay. They had already approached Charles for what he could give. Now it looked as if they had paid Francis a direct call.

On the pretext of reaching for more toast, I perused him more closely. There was a puffiness to his features, as if he had not slept well. And his eyes ... With a shock, I realised he was frightened. Despite knowing he was bad, I felt a quick sympathy steal through me. Whoever had roughed him up had threatened him. They must have. It wasn't enough to bruise his face, he must know that they were coming back. And that they wanted their money.

It was during the main course that Charles dropped his bombshell. The ham was roasted to perfection, and Peggy's cut vegetables provided a tasty glazed side dish along with a mound of roasted potatoes. Mrs Bell had done well: I doubted

I'd have room for the dessert at this rate.

There was none of Francis's lazy teasing with his aunt tonight. He contributed little to the light conversation led by Lady Anne. She in turn tried to eke out of him some chatter on this and that, while Charles chipped in about the new horses he had purchased. I did not speak much either, but that was because I did not feel it was my place to do so. If asked for my opinion on the country gossip or the weather, then I made some bland response. My mind was too tuned to the guest, and how Charles' plan was playing out.

At last, Lady Anne ran out of suitable conversational topics. Charles stared at his plate. There was only the sound of our cutlery chinking on the china. The butler came and poured more wine. A log in the fire suddenly dropped, and the noise was startlingly loud. Francis seemed oblivious to all this. There was little wrong with his appetite. He had managed to put away three helpings of Mrs Bell's huge ham and trimmings. I noticed he was on his third glass of wine, too. His face was increasingly ruddy. By contrast, Charles sipped at his single glass, and mine was untouched.

'Ah, you might be interested to hear this …' Charles said casually, just as the silence became unbearable.

'What might that be?' Francis said, sounding uninterested. He shoved a final forkful of ham into his mouth and chewed.

I averted my gaze. I had no wish to see masticated food in his open mouth. His manners were quite appalling.

'There is a local geological society starting up. It sounds fascinating. They are interested in all sorts of different rocks; and fossicking, too.'

'Really.' Francis put down his cutlery and patted his protruding stomach. He belched and Lady Anne winced.

Now in came the frothy creation that was dessert. We waited until plates of it were in front of us, and the servants once more out of sight.

'The head of the society came to see

me,' Charles went on as if there had been no interruption. 'He was looking for a place to take the group as a first outing. I thought of the caves down at the beach and recommended them to him. He was very grateful. I believe their first outing is tomorrow afternoon, and I look forward to hearing their news.'

There was a loud crack as Francis's fork shattered the meringue on his plate. Pieces of it flew onto the tablecloth. Lady Anne looked shocked — whether at her nephew's dessert *faux pas* or at her son's news, it wasn't clear.

Francis made his excuses soon after. Lady Anne tried to persuade him to stay for an evening of cards or singing at the pianoforte, but he declared his weariness and desire for an early night. His carriage was soon speeding down the driveway and gone from sight.

'That went well,' Charles whispered to me. 'Now all we have to do is be ready.'

'You think he will go to the caves tonight?' I whispered back.

Lady Anne had retired, but we were

standing in the hall by the dining room, with servants tidying up and moving the dinner dishes and otherwise readying Bowerly for late evening.

'I'm convinced of it,' Charles said. 'Meet me in an hour in the walled garden. Go quietly, and don't let yourself be seen by anyone. I want an answer tonight. If Francis has betrayed his family honour, then ...' He didn't finish what he was going to say. Instead, his jaw tightened ominously. 'Go,' he said.

I hurried away from him, and upstairs to prepare. I had no idea what the night would bring. But I knew I had to be ready for anything.

I was wrapped up well in several layers of petticoats under my thickest skirt, and my legs felt no cold. My upper body was equally warm with my woollen shawl snug over my coat. My bonnet kept the worst of the weather from my head. It was not raining, but there was a heaviness to the air, as if the damp might turn to water droplets at any moment. There was only the sound of my skirt swishing through the grasses and the pounding of my heart as I went to meet Charles.

'Good timekeeping,' he remarked in a low tone as I approached, and I heard approval in his voice.

He needed have no fear that I was not capable of the task ahead, whatever it was. I was resolved to do my best to help him. I was not only punctual, but calm and determined, with my fear suppressed. Francis did not seem a violent man — but who knew what a trapped creature would do? I had heard tales of foxes chewing off their own legs to escape the snare. If a man was desperate to escape justice, then what might *he* do …?

I tried not to think about that.

'Are you ready?' Charles asked.

I nodded, and then realised he couldn't see me.

'Yes, quite ready.'

'Then let us proceed. We will walk to the caves as quietly as possible, and then wait in the darkness until Francis arrives.'

'You're certain, then, that it is he?'

'Sadly, I have indeed come to that

conclusion; but as I told you, I will not make any charges or decisions until I have seen him with my own eyes. Mrs Bell may not be telling the truth. After all, she has her own skin to save.'

'Are you sure he will come tonight?'

'Once he heard my story about the geological society, he was quick to leave. I told him the group would be exploring the caves tomorrow afternoon. That only leaves tonight under cover of darkness for him to remove the stolen goods. Believe me, Amelia, I will be only too relieved if we find no-one tonight. If that is the case, then it can't be Francis who is to blame.'

I could barely make out his outline in the darkness of the walled garden — only just sufficiently to know that he had turned and was making his way to the meadows. The moon cast a feeble silver light and I was able to follow.

The crash and boom of the sea was audible. In the moonlight, the water was simply a black band against the streaky sky and scattered stars.

'The sea is close,' Charles warned as we

descended the now-familiar stone steps. 'But it is on the turn, so there should be no danger of being trapped at the cliffs.'

'Thank goodness.'

'Are you afraid? Do you wish to go home? I should not have asked you to accompany me. What on earth was I thinking of —?'

'No, no, I am quite alright,' I said quickly. I did not want to miss out on this adventure. 'I'm not scared at all.' This was a small exaggeration of the truth, but no matter. How could I let Charles go alone into possible danger? If something befell him and I had walked away, I couldn't have lived with my conscience.

'Very well then, Miss Thorne, let us go forwards.' There was his warm humour now, and I felt close to him.

'Where shall we hide?' I whispered as we grew close to the cave mouths.

'The moon is casting large shadows so we may wait in them,' he said, 'Over by the bluff. It's far away that he won't see us and near enough that we will hear him coming.'

We stood with our backs to the rocks and waited. After a while my back began to ache. I rubbed the small of it with my fingers. It was getting colder too. With no exercise to warm the blood it was difficult to stay comfortable. Beside me, Charles was an immobile shape. He seemed able to wait without movement, like a panther awaiting its prey.

'What if he was already in the cave when we arrived?' I said as this thought popped up.

'Then we will catch him coming out.' Came the calm but muted reply.

Charles was way ahead of me. I felt stupid for the remark. I wriggled. Standing still for so long was painful. The tide had sucked and rasped its way fairly far out again as we'd waited. Suddenly Charles swore softly under his breath.

'What is it?' I said.

'We've been here for hours,' he whispered back. 'Francis should either have arrived or have come back out of the cave by now. I'm a fool. Don't you see?'

'What do you mean?' But even as I

formed the question, I realised what he meant.

Charles straightened up and took a step out from the rocks. He turned to me.

'I mean that there must be another way into the caves. I've been an idiot. Think about it, Amelia. How did Francis get all the stolen goods, the heavy candlesticks, the large and unwieldy pictures down here? He'd never manage them on those cliff steps.'

'We've had a wasted journey,' I said in dismay, 'We've lost our chance to surprise him.'

Charles walked swiftly to the caves. I ran after him.

'I want you to go home now,' he said.

'No, I'm coming with you.'

'No, you're not. It's too dangerous. I'm going into the cave, and I'll either find Francis in the end chamber, or I'll discover another way out and follow it to him. Either way, I don't want you to get in the middle of what might be a struggle. It's one thing to watch for him out here in the open, and quite another to confront him in an enclosed space within the cave system.'

I made some small sound of protest and he put up both palms to stop me.

'Please, Amelia. I must go, I'm losing time. You'll be perfectly safe walking back to the house.' And with that, he went into the cave, leaving me behind.

I stood there for a moment. A rush of anger flooded me. How dared he! He had taken me with him so far, and then abandoned me. Never mind that he believed it to be in my best interests, and for my safety — it wasn't good enough.

I let a few minutes go past, and then I entered the cave.

I went as silently as possible. I could see the faint light of a candle some distance in front. Of course, Charles needed it, otherwise there was a danger of stumbling into the walls. I hoped fervently that Francis would not see it. When I reached the wide chamber, Charles was gone.

I cannot describe the depth of darkness that surrounded me. I held up my hand in front of my face and was unable to see it. I tried to visualise the chamber. I had seen it before in candlelight when I found Francis's hoard. Then I had gone straight to the centre to see what was there. My best plan of action now was to touch the rough stone beside me and circle the edge until I found the other exit.

Carefully, keeping my hand firmly on the stone, I began to step to the left. It had to be done slowly. If there was a rut or pothole in the ground, I did not want to be flung into it. I was ever-conscious that Charles was already ahead by minutes. I didn't want to lose him.

I continued on my circle until a little after halfway, when my hand fell into nothing. A cold draught blew at me. Here was the other way in and out of the cave. Charles was right. We had been foolish not to think of this. The passage curved up almost immediately. There was an odour of wet earth. I moved faster now, desperate to get up to the surface. Where was Charles?

A blast of cold night air hit me. I was there. The way out was fringed with roots and crumbling soil. I pushed past them. As my senses adjusted, I saw the scene unfolding beyond. Two figures struggling. Three horses, restless, tied to the trunk of a tree. All around was woodland. As I watched helplessly, one figure broke free, ran for the horses and mounted. The second figure, who I guessed was Charles by his height, ran after him and leapt onto a second horse to gallop after the first. Two bulky bags had dropped from the horse as he went.

What was I to do? The sensible action was to go right that instant for help. But Charles didn't want interference until he'd caught his cousin. What if Francis overpowered him? I shook my head impatiently. Charles was taller, stronger and more athletic than Francis by far.

I approached the last horse. He was twitching with nerves. There were bags slung over his back. Murmuring gently, I stroked his nose until he calmed. Then I managed to undo the bags. They slid to the ground. I got onto the horse. There was nothing for it but to ride with my skirts hitched. Thank goodness it was night and no-one there to see.

Then I turned him and pressed my heels to his flanks, urging him to follow his companions. We rushed through the trees. Branches snatched at my bonnet. With stiff fingers, I loosened the ribbons and threw it off. Rather that than I should be strangled by it. Now the branches grabbed my hair. No matter. Soon we were out of the woods and onto the fields.

The others had made headway. As I watched, the figures merged and collided. Then they parted around scrub. Once more one rider brought his mount alongside the other. It was strange. There was no shouting. Nothing but the whistling wind, the galloping hooves and the screech of a night owl.

I kept pace. The landscape became familiar. We had come in an enormous loop. We were galloping towards the cliffs. Not those near the beach with the caves, but further on past the vicarage and the village houses. Towards the beach that Peggy had described to me. Here the cliffs were not so high. I made out pale silhouettes of dunes and marram.

A sudden sharp cry made my heart squeeze. With horror I saw a horse and rider veer too close to the edge. In a second the other followed. Both figures disappeared from sight over the cliffs.

'Charles!' I screamed.

I slid from my horse and ran to the edge. Sick to the stomach, I peered over. It wasn't far to the shingle below but there what I saw made me cry out again. The horses had cantered off along the beach, leaving the two figures prone and still.

At that very moment I realised I had fallen in love with Charles. He was a Viscount, a powerful and wealthy man so far above me but I didn't care. *I loved him*. And I had to get to him. Was he alive?

I scrambled down the rocks. Thorny brambles snagged at me. My breath was coming shallow and fast. As I got to them, one of the men sat up and groaned.

'Charles?'

'What the devil are you doing here?'

came the annoyed response.

My chest eased in delight.

'I told you distinctly to go home. Why aren't you safely back at Bowerly?'

'Never mind that. Are you hurt?' I said briskly, to hide the joy I felt knowing he was alive.

'A few bruises but apart from that I'm fine. I'm more concerned about Francis.'

So it was Francis Williams. Although we had been fairly certain he was the thief, it was still disappointing to have it confirmed. How awful for Charles and Lady Anne. What shame this would bring to a proud family.

'Let me see him,' I said, brushing past the Viscount to crouch beside Francis.

He was unconscious but breathing. I felt for broken bones and could find none.

'I think he is simply stunned,' I said at last. 'What are you going to do?'

'I know what you would have me do,' he replied, 'but I am not going to call the constable.'

'What then? Is your cousin to get away

with his crimes?'

'I must think of my mother and my aunt. The shock of the scandal would be too much for them. I must protect Bowerly too, with all that I have. If news of this gets out into the county, we will never lift our heads for shame.'

'I understand what you're saying but … is he to get away scot-free?' I felt my indignation rising on behalf of all the victims that Francis Williams had robbed. Yet I understood entirely what Charles meant. If justice was done, then Lady Anne and Mrs Williams would become victims too.

'Francis will pay in some measure for the anguish he has caused,' Charles said grimly. 'Come, help me raise him up. We cannot rest here for the night. Then we must gather up the horses and go back for the saddle bags.'

Yes, there was much to do before dawn broke. I have never been so exhausted in my life. Somehow we sat Francis up and brought him to waking. He complained of a terrible headache but otherwise appeared healthy. The horses had stopped to graze on the dune grasses. I approached them on tiptoe and soon was able to bring them back to the two men.

Then came the tricky journey back to the woodlands. Francis had maintained a sulky silence. Charles and I ignored him but kept his horse between ours in case he made a bolt for freedom.

Once in the woodlands, we came to a halt. Charles took the reins of my horse and I dismounted. He tied all three horses to the tree.

'I want you to go home now,' he said, 'and this time I want no argument. Please?'

I yawned reflexively.

'You have done admirably,' Charles said softly. He reached his hand to me and my breath stopped.

But he didn't touch me. He pulled his fingers back and stiffened his posture.

'Your hair is wild.'

'I'm sorry ... I lost my bonnet in the woods.'

'Don't apologise, it looks … well, it's time you went. I have much to do before I can return to Bowerly.'

'What will you do?'

'You must go,' he repeated more firmly.

I turned then and walked through the trees, barely seeing the pale birch bark, the gnarled oaks and the angular bones of the ancient limes. Just where the trees fringed the fields, I glanced back. Charles and Francis were just visible. What was he going to do? It was not my place to interfere further. I was simply the governess to his child. When it came to it, I had to obey his wishes.

12

I awoke in my bed quite disorientated. A watery sun trickled in. My breath showed white. The fire had not been lit. When I tried to sit up my muscles shrieked. All the activity of the previous night was being paid for.

There was a quiet knock at the door and Peggy stuck her head in.

'Are you awake? Shall I make up the fire?'

'Yes please. What time is it?'

'Oh, it's early yet. Did you sleep well?'

'Like a log,' I lied. 'Is breakfast served?'

'I think so. His Lordship is up and about. Lady Anne is having breakfast in bed. Mary is still asleep so you can rest for a while if you want to.'

Peggy got the fire blazing nicely. She moved round the room, tidying as she went. I tried to wake up fully.

'I'll bring you up some hot water.'

'Thank you Peggy, you're very good to me.'

She looked surprised, 'I'm only doing my job, you know. Mrs Dane said I was to make sure you had your comforts. She's taken to you all right. You've got a place here now, a good home and you deserve it. Edna and Lil are that grateful you cared for them when they was ill.'

'I was very glad to be able to help.'

Mary was in a buoyant mood when I went into the nursery.

'Papa has promised to bring me a new painting set back from London. Think what lovely pictures we can make together, Amelia.' She clapped her hands happily.

'When is your father going to London?' I tried to keep my dismay hidden.

My emotions regarding the Viscount were in turmoil. I was deeply in love with him. I couldn't change the way I felt. But I knew nothing could come of it. He loved Catherine, and I could not rival a dead woman. And I had to remember my place socially. No, it was hopeless and the sooner I came to terms with that, the better it would be. I would have peace. My destiny was to be a spinster. At least I had employment, and I loved Mary as if she was my own flesh and blood.

'He's going today,' Mary said. 'He came to say goodbye and that's when he promised me so many nice presents when he returns.'

When will that be? I didn't ask the child. It was wrong to question her so. I was disappointed and hurt that Charles had not said goodbye to me before leaving. Did I mean so little to him? Yes, that was so, I said harshly to myself. I had to believe it. What a nonsense that Viscount Bowerly of Bowerly Hall should seek out the governess to say farewell. I thought of all we had shared the previous evening. There were secrets. He trusted me to keep them safe and I would.

'We will begin our lessons today with a piece of poetry,' I said. 'Now be a good girl and take out your book and open it to page four.'

I set her to learning the small poem

and went downstairs. I had to see for myself that he had gone. I was in luck. The Viscount's carriage had pulled up at the driveway. As I stepped outside, Charles arrived. The butler was busy ordering the footmen to stow the luggage. In the middle of all the preparations, Charles took me to one side.

'I must go to London on urgent business. Will you be here when I return?'

'Of course. I will be teaching Mary as usual. She is very excited about the gifts you will be bringing back.'

He smiled. 'Such an easy way to a child's heart, is it not?'

'She loves you whether you give her a painting set or not.'

I was dying to ask him what had become of Francis but could not. Lady Anne came out of the house. I moved back to let her embrace her son.

'When will you return?' she asked.

'I will be away no longer than a fortnight,' he said.

'I do hope the weather remains mild,' Lady Anne fretted. 'Storms will only delay you.'

'There is no need to worry,' Charles said. 'I will be back soon. You have Mrs Dane to keep the house in order and Amelia to keep you company.'

He met my gaze above her head. I nodded my promise. I'd look after Lady Anne and keep her entertained.

'What of Mary? She will miss you awfully.'

'I have to go,' he said gently, and took his arm from hers.

As he passed me he spoke in a low voice so that only I could hear.

'All is in order.'

That was it. But it was sufficient that I knew he had dealt with the problem of Francis. I watched as his carriage went down the long driveway and around the bend. I missed him already.

'Please join me for dinner tonight,' Lady Anne said. 'I will be quite lonely without him. We will talk more of your mother.'

'Thank you, I look forward to that.'

After we had learned our poetry and Mary had spent an hour with her grandmamma I helped her to dress warmly.

'Would you like to play with Charlotte?' I asked her, tying her ribbons under her chin.

'Yes please, Amelia. I haven't seen her in ages. I want to tell her about my new painting set. Can she come and paint with us once Papa is home?'

I assured her that she could invite Charlotte to do just that. We hurried over to the vicarage, both eager to see our friends. Sarah looked well. She welcomed us warmly. Charlotte took Mary upstairs to play with her dolls' house while I was taken into the drawing room.

'How are you?' I said.

'Engaged.' Sarah stifled a giggle.

'Congratulations. How marvellous. When is the happy day?'

'Our engagement is not made public so far,' Sarah said. 'I want to write to my cousins and their families first. James has an uncle who has been very kind to him but who is travelling in Europe so he wishes to wait until Uncle Jeremy has the news.'

'Your father must be delighted.'

'Yes, he is very happy for us both. Oh, Amelia, I'm in seventh heaven. I laugh out loud for no good reason and I find myself humming little tunes. Is it wrong to be so happy?'

'No of course not. You must enjoy every minute. I wish you both the best of happiness.'

'I hope you find love as I have done,' Sarah said, giving me a fierce hug.

I had no answer to that so I changed the subject to ask if there was any county news.

'News of the greatest import,' she said. 'I should have told you right away except that my own news was even more exciting. Did you know that all the stolen belongings have been returned to the great houses?'

'Really?' That was news. Charles had acted swiftly. I knew that the staff at Bowerly Hall were very fond of him and it was no stretch of the imagination to think that his workers would help him in this and keep their tongues still.

'Yes, this very morning at break of dawn, apparently. All the paintings and ornaments and so forth left at their doors. Who can have done it? Perhaps the thief has shown his remorse.'

'Quite possibly.' And what of Francis? Where was he? I was very certain he had not returned the goods.

'Goodness, where are my manners? I have not offered you any refreshments. Will you take some tea and cake?'

We returned to the Hall in late afternoon having had a lovely time with Sarah and Charlotte. As we went inside, a footman passed me a letter which had arrived for me at midday. I did not open it. I did not receive much mail and I wanted to savour it alone. I forgot about it while I played the pianoforte with Mary and then took dinner with Lady Anne.

Only once I was getting ready for bed did I remember it and took it out to read.

My dearest Amelia
I hope this letter finds you well. I en-
joyed your descriptions of Bowerly Hall

209

*and its gardens. A lot has happened
since I wrote to you last.*

*I think I mentioned my travels to care
for my cousin. She was very poorly and
sadly has since passed away. It came
as rather a shock as she had appeared
to be improving. Her heart was weak,
poor Clara, and the physician said
that nothing could have saved her. He
praised my constant attentions to her.
I do miss her.*

*However, that is not why I am writing
to you. After Clara died, I had a lot to
do in my own house as I had rather ne-
glected it to care for her. I had adjusted
with relief to not having to journey
each day to the other side of London
when I was called to a reading of her
will. It was most unusual and I was
inclined not to go. I am rather tired at
present. It has been an emotional few
months. However, in the end, I did go
to listen to the lawyer. I felt it was only
fair to Clara to do so.*

*It came as rather a shock to discover
that Clara has left me everything. Her*

beautiful house and its pretty gardens. Her carriage and horses. And rather a large amount of money.

My dear, I am writing to offer you a home at last. You will have no need of employment ever again. I felt terrible when you came to me that I could not offer you permanent shelter. Your mother was such a true friend and I wanted so much to care for her only daughter. Well, now I can.

Please, Amelia, come and live with me. You will want for nothing and your companionship will give me great pleasure.

Yours

Hannah Bidens

I laid the letter down on my bed. It was hard to adjust to what Mrs Bidens had written. I was so very pleased for her. She was a kind and generous woman and now she was financially secure for life. She wanted me to share in her bounty. I could give up work. I need never have to fear the future again. But what turmoil her letter had stirred!

I got up and paced the room. Ten steps to the wall, spin and ten steps to the other. Repeat. Mrs Bidens was lonely and tired. She needed me. I should go. But Mary needed me too. I loved her and the thought of leaving her was painful. Then there was Charles. I loved him in quite a different way. Even if it was useless. I couldn't bear not seeing him again. But what future was there in loving him?

The next morning I was worn out. There were dark circles under my eyes and Peggy commented upon them. I told her about Mrs Bidens' letter and her kind offer. Peggy's mouth turned into an 'O' of surprise.

'Well, ain't you the lucky one. When will you leave?' She stared at me and shook her head dismally. 'You're considering turning her down, aren't you?'

'I've grown to love Bowerly and I'm very fond of Mary, of all of you. I just … I don't know what to do for the best, Peggy.'

'Well I'll tell you then.' Peggy stuck her hands on her hips as if to give me a lecture. 'It's all very well working for the gentry but you've got to remember that's what it is. It's work. We're not part of the family. They don't care about us really. If they didn't need you, they'd give you notice tomorrow. That's the plain truth. What about when Mary's older? They won't keep you on out of charity, you know. Grab your chance, Amelia, grab it with both hands. It's a rare thing you're being offered. Imagine, not having to work ever again.' She sighed, picked up her pail and duster and walked away, still shaking her head.

I felt chastised. The more I thought about it, the more I began to see that Peggy was right. It struck me that I would be an embarrassment to Charles if he ever suspected my feelings for him. Could I hide my love so easily? I felt not. It was bound to show eventually. Humiliation would surely follow.

I decided I had to leave before he returned from London. Lady Anne's prediction on the weather had come true. Late autumn storms had blown in and would make travelling unpredictable. The worst part was leaving Mary. It was going to rip my heart out.

'Are you unhappy here?' Lady Anne said when I went to tell her my decision.

'On the contrary, I have had some of my happiest hours in your house,' I said honestly.

'But you want to leave us.'

'I have had a very kind offer from Mrs Bidens of a loving home and I feel she is lonely too.'

'What about Mary? She will be distraught when you go. She has become very fond of you.'

'As I am of her. But she is young and she will soon forget me.' Which was a sad thought in itself.

'Very well, I can see you have quite made up your mind and that I will not be able to persuade you otherwise. You do realise you have left me in a difficult position. Mary will have no teacher if you go now. Can you not stay a month or two longer? What is the rush?'

I could hardly tell her I wanted to avoid

her son. *Will you be here when I return?* he had asked me. Had he had some premonition that I'd be gone? Like Mary, he'd soon forget me. So I shut down my emotions and packed up my bags.

Mary cried as I left Bowerly Hall. She clutched at the doll I had bought for her in the village. It wasn't much but it was all I could buy at short notice. I had sent a letter to Sarah, wishing her well for her wedding and future life. I hadn't wanted to visit and have to bear yet more farewells. A chapter in my life was ending. A new one in London was to begin. I was doing the right thing, wasn't I?

13

Mrs Bidens was overjoyed to see me. She had not moved address despite inheriting her cousin's house.

'Oh no, it's far too large for me to rattle about in. I can't leave this house where Arthur and I started our married life together. Too many memories. Now drink up your tea, you look a bit peaky. Are you well?'

I had been back in London for several weeks. At first I dreamed that Charles would find me and beg me to return with him to Bowerly. As the days passed so did that dream. I was no young girl with foolish notions. I was a woman getting too old to think of matrimony. I devoted myself to Mrs Bidens' comforts. She had been persuaded to take on another maid and to increase her cook's hours to full time. She had no housekeeper so I took on much of the role.

'You've taken on too much,' she said. 'I shouldn't have allowed you to organise the house and plan the meals. I shall employ a house keeper after all.'

'Don't do that, please. I enjoy keeping busy.' The busier I was, the better. It stopped me missing Charles and Mary with every second of the day.

'Very well, if you are sure. I thought perhaps we might go shopping for material? There is a very good seamstress I know of who can run up the latest fashions.'

'Dear Hannah, you are too good to me.'

'Not at all. I enjoy being able to treat you, it gives me great pleasure. Shall we plan to go into the city this week?'

She went out that morning as there was much to do with settling her cousin's estate. I decided to re-organise the linens. It was just the sort of simple task that soothed my brain. To be honest I was restless. I missed organising Mary's lessons. It wasn't the same, reading poetry by myself. I longed to discuss it with someone. Hannah was not a great reader, by her own admission.

I opened the linen cupboard and pulled out great piles of towels, tablecloths, napkins and other odds and ends. There was plenty to do. This task looked likely to take all day. I was right in the middle of it when the doorbell rang. Hannah's new maid answered. There was some short conversation and I vaguely wondered who the caller was. We did not get many social calls. Of course the butcher, coal merchant and others came to the back door.

'There's a gentleman here to see you, miss,' Agnes said.

'Oh, please tell him Mrs Bidens is not at home. If he will leave a message ...'

'He asked for you. For Miss Thorne, he says.'

Puzzled, I stood up from my position kneeling in a froth of linens. Uncle Timothy came to mind. I had written to my uncle and aunt to let them know I was back in London. They had not replied. Perhaps Uncle Timothy was visiting in person. There was a pit in my stomach as I went to the door. However, I pasted on a smile. I might not like my relatives but that didn't mean I should be unkind and unwelcoming.

It was not Uncle Timothy. It was Charles. All broad shoulders, well-fitting jacket and immaculate breeches, high polished black boots and … and … Oh his dear, familiar dark scowl and piercing blue gaze.

'Devil take it, Amelia. What made you leave?' he said savagely.

'And a wonderfully good day to you too, sir.'

That took the wind from his sails. He removed his hat and came inside without waiting for an invitation. My whole body was singing a melody as I showed him into Hannah's newly decorated drawing room. I called Agnes and asked for tea. I had not thought to see Charles ever again and now he was here.

'Mary is moping horribly.' He sat on the nearest armchair and stared at me accusingly.

I perched on the edge of the other chair, conscious of his knees so close to mine.

'Is she keeping up with her painting? Has she been practising her poetry?' What a pang it gave me to ask these things. In my mind, I saw the little girl and it twisted at my heart. I hoped she was not lonely and that Charlotte was allowed to visit.

'Why don't you come back and ask her yourself?' Charles said.

'I can't.'

He sprang up, making me jump. How tall he was. He made Hannah's lovely room appear small as he paced it.

'If there's something to say, please simply do so. Stop wearing a hole in the new carpet,' I said rather sharply as my nerves tingled.

'The thing is, Amelia …' He stopped and coughed then began again. 'The thing is, it isn't only Mary who's moping.'

Did I let a tiny ray of hope slip into my heart at that very moment?

'Please do go on,' I said calmly while

my fingers tightened on my dress folds.

'I miss you. I need you to come back to Bowerly with me.'

'I have a home here now. Hannah, that is Mrs Bidens, has kindly given me a place to live.'

'Is it enough? I believed you to love Bowerly Hall. Do you prefer London?' He frowned. 'Because if you do, then we will live here. I have a town house.'

'What are you asking of me?'

He grasped my hands in his and I felt the thrill of that contact. His were large and capable and strong and the touch of them did something odd to my nerves and my insides.

'I am asking you to marry me, Miss Amelia Thorne. To do me the honour of becoming my wife. You are the bravest, most determined and most beautiful woman I have met and I can't live without you.'

'You can't marry me — what would people say? I was a governess.'

'You are no longer a governess,' he reminded me. 'You are a lady of quality, living a genteel life.'

'But you could have anyone. You can take your pick of the debutantes.' I felt I had to remind him that I was not a young lady fresh from the school room.

He brushed that aside with a scornful expression. 'What do I want with a silly young girl. I want a woman who'll follow me into danger to save me. I want a woman who loves my daughter as much as I do. A kind, generous and loving companion for all our years. Put me out of my misery and tell me yes!'

'Why have you waited all these weeks to find me?' I had to ask. I didn't wish to prolong his unease but I had to know.

He nodded as if he understood. 'I wanted to come to you immediately. It was an agony to wait but there were matters that had to be concluded. As you know, I journeyed to London. After I left Bowerly, I went to pick up Francis. From there we travelled to the docks in the city where I had booked a cabin and passage to America for him. He is now working there for a friend of mine until he has paid back all his debts. In return, I have decided not to expose him for his crimes. It will bring nothing but ill fortune for my mother and his in terms of society. Then of course, it has taken me some weeks to placate my aunt who misses him. I have also had to arrange financial matters for her and for the men that Francis owes money to. I'm sorry it has taken so much time. Finally, I am here on my own selfish matters of the heart.'

'Are you certain about this?' I asked. I did not want him to regret his choice in me. 'What will people say when they hear you are to marry a woman who has no title and no wealth?'

'I don't care one whit,' he said. 'I have wealth enough for us. Besides, Mary told me not to return home without you. She can be quite severe.'

I had barely the words of agreement and love spoken when my mouth was claimed by his.

14

It was many months before Anne, my new mother-in-law, felt able to unburden herself. We had settled nicely into a gentle friendship and she was very happy to hear that Charles and I were to marry. The wedding was not a grand affair. There were some people who were shocked that the Viscount Bowerly was to wed the woman who had been governess in the Hall. It was circulated that I was penniless and a gold digger by a few society ladies in London.

We ignored all the gossip. The villagers and the staff at Bowerly were all delighted with our news and that was enough for us. Charles declared he had no intention to go to London for the season. He much preferred country living. I was happy to be where he was.

Hannah Bidens was contented too. Although sad to see me go she was pleased I was to marry. We had found her a new companion, an older maiden lady who suited Hannah very well. Together they took small trips to museums and gracious gardens and the theatre. We wrote often to each other.

As the Viscountess, I was able to help Lady Anne with the everyday running of Bowerly Hall and take some of the more onerous tasks from her. One of those tasks was the preparation of the weekly menu. Anne confided in me that she found dealing with Mrs Bell quite horrid. I didn't much like it either but since we shared a secret to her detriment she was polite and deferential.

Still, no-one was as relieved as I when one day she announced she was retiring to live with her cousin in another village further north. Charles provided a generous sum of money as a goodbye gesture and she went away content and without a bad word for anyone. The new cook, Mrs Freeman, was younger and much jollier. Peggy told me she was instantly taken to the heart of all the staff.

Mary was ecstatic that her father and I had fallen in love. She made a beautiful flower girl at our wedding, scattering pink rose petals before us as we walked up the aisle in the ancient church on the Bowerly estate.

She hugged me tightly after the ceremony.

'Can I ask you something please, Amelia?'

'You can ask me anything you wish,' I said with a smile and kissed her soft cheek.

'May I ... may I call you Mama?'

I hadn't expected that. My eyes were shiny as I replied, 'I love you as if you were my own daughter and I should like it very well to be called Mama.'

She paused, her brow creased in thought, before she gazed up at me, 'You know I shall never forget my real mama, it's just that I only have a picture of her and I never knew her. She won't mind if she shares me with you, will she?'

'No darling, I don't think she'll mind one little bit. I expect she's looking down at you from heaven right this minute and she's glad because you are happy.'

Mary nodded and skipped away to play with Charlotte out on the lawn at the front of the church.

It was later in the season when Anne decided to talk. We were sitting in the drawing room, a warm fire crackling in the hearth and our concentration intent on our embroidery. Charles had excused himself to work in his study. He was about to buy more horses for the stables and of course the estate did not run itself. Mary was in bed and her new governess had retired to her suite.

'Charles has told me that Francis will not be returning to England,' Anne said suddenly.

I glanced at her but her gaze was downcast upon the circle of colourful threads. Her fingers flew as she sewed a neat flower of red.

'Oh, that is news to me,' I said, surprised my husband had not told me. 'I thought his intention was to return after his journeys.'

Anne put down her embroidery and sighed. She looked straight at me. I put down the silken threads I had been attempting to untangle and gave her my full attention.

'We both know that Francis did not go to America of his own free will,' she said, 'although I do believe that he has decided to stay there because he has a future which he may not have here.'

'You know about the break in at Bowerly? And that Francis was the thief who stole from houses across the county?'

She nodded. 'I always had my suspicions about him but I didn't know the truth at the time. I prayed that he was not to blame and I am guilty of avoiding the unpleasantness of it. I am quite aware of my nephew's shortcomings but I am terribly fond of him. I love Charles of course. I am his mother and that is a bond that cannot be broken. But Charles can be very serious and Francis was ever more light-hearted and charming. He is a foil to my son.'

'I see.'

'It's hard to explain,' Anne said. 'I felt there was something wrong but I suppose I wanted to believe that Francis's money problems would be solved … that he would find a way to make his land pay or to manage his inheritance better.'

'Did you know about the caves?'

'I didn't know he had taken things and kept them there. But I knew he spent hours there. That's why I tried to deflect you from going to the beach.'

Anne had been the face at the window that I had glimpsed, I realised.

'I was nervous when he came to dinner and wanted to speak with Mrs Bell,' Anne went on. 'It didn't make sense. He didn't know her that well. If I had known he was going to break into our home I don't know what I would have done.'

I didn't blame Anne for any of this. She had done nothing wrong except love her nephew and ignore her instincts. As for Mrs Williams, Francis's mother, Charles had explained that she did know what her son was doing. Her hysteria in church was pure guilt. She was greedy for the money Francis was going to make from his crimes yet her conscience pricked at her.

It was harder to forgive her but we did, for the sake of the family. We invited her to Bowerly to dine but as yet she had not accepted, giving her poor health as an excuse. I knew that Charles made sure she was looked after, in Francis's absence.

Another year passed quickly until it was once more summer. Sarah came to visit bringing her new baby boy.

'You're decorating the Hall,' she said, handing Jeremy over to me for a cuddle.

'Yes, we are. It's a massive task, but we've hired locally from the village where it is much-needed work, so we're pleased to do so. How is Jeremy?'

'Teething, poor darling, so he's rather grumpy. James keeps asking me when he might take his son fishing. I tell him he may when the lad can walk, which will be a while yet,' Sarah laughed.

Marriage and motherhood suited her well. She and James were frequent visitors to our home and we were likewise often at the vicarage for afternoon tea or a pleasant evening of food and music.

Peggy knocked and came in.

'Oh, look you, master Jem. You'd like one of Mrs Freeman's biscuits, wouldn't you, young man? Shall I take him downstairs, Milady?'

'That would be lovely,' Sarah said gratefully. 'He does like being spoiled by everyone.'

Peggy took the baby with her and we heard her singing to him on her way. She was singing a lot recently as she had become engaged to one of the footmen and was looking forward to her own wedding. Charles and I discussed what we would give the couple as a wedding gift. Peggy didn't know it but she was soon to be the owner of a dear little cottage on the estate with its own piece of land and the option of fields to rent. Her fiancé, although a footman, was of farming stock and eager to keep a few cattle and tend crops and I thought that Peggy could have a very good future if all turned out as we hoped for her.

Charles came to me after Sarah had left that afternoon. He kissed me tenderly and I felt the tingle of attraction that only intensified the longer I knew him.

'Did Sarah approve of the alterations to the entrance hall?'

'She liked the new colour scheme immensely,' I said. 'I fear for James as it has quite put in her the mood to refresh her own house.'

'Did you show her the rest of the re-decorating?' my husband asked with a quirked brow.

I walked with him upstairs to the bedroom next to ours. The walls had been stripped of old wall paper and the old furniture removed. There was no-one there as the workmen had stopped for the day. A pot of pale lemon paint stood on the floorboards.

'No, I didn't mention this to Sarah,' I said, leaning comfortably in to his side. 'I wanted to keep our very good news all to ourselves for now.' I reached up on tip toe to kiss him.

Charles smiled and put his hand gently

on my stomach.

'We'll tell Mary tomorrow about her new brother or sister.'

Yes, I agreed, we'd tell Mary and Anne too, and together as a family we would celebrate in our good fortune at Bowerly Hall.

We do hope that you have enjoyed reading this large print book.

Did you know that all of our titles are available for purchase?

We publish a wide range of high quality large print books including:
Romances, Mysteries, Classics
General Fiction
Non Fiction and Westerns

Special interest titles available in large print are:
The Little Oxford Dictionary
Music Book, Song Book
Hymn Book, Service Book

Also available from us courtesy of Oxford University Press:
Young Readers' Dictionary
(large print edition)
Young Readers' Thesaurus
(large print edition)

For further information or a free brochure, please contact us at:
Ulverscroft Large Print Books Ltd.,
The Green, Bradgate Road, Anstey,
Leicester, LE7 7FU, England.
Tel: (00 44) **0116 236 4325**
Fax: (00 44) **0116 234 0205**